Judith Heide Gilliland

STRANGE BIRDS

Melanie Kroupa Books
Farrar, Straus and Giroux · New York

www.fsgkidsbooks.com

Library of Congress Cataloging-in-Publication Data
Gilliland, Judith Heide.
Strange birds / by Judith Heide Gilliland.— 1st ed.
    p.   cm.
Summary: With her parents lost at sea, eleven-year-old Anna finds
comfort in a tree with magical properties which suddenly becomes
home to some amazing creatures who may need her help.
ISBN-13: 978-0-374-37275-0
ISBN-10: 0-374-37275-6
[1. Horses—Fiction. 2. Magic—Fiction. 3. Trees—Fiction.]
I. Title.

PZ7.G4155 Str 2006
[Fic]—dc22

                                              2005045072

For my twin, Roxy
and our best friend, Beth—
and the horses we rode

PART 1

THE DIFFERENCE BETWEEN MONDAY AND TUESDAY

On Monday Anna Farrington was a perfectly happy child. It was almost her eleventh birthday, and on that day her dream would come true: her parents were giving her a horse! She would ride him every day; she would brush his coat and feed him. Together they would trot down forest paths and canter across fields. They would be best friends.

This particular Monday was made even more delicious by the fact that she was sleeping at her friend Beth's house while her parents were away on a sailing trip. That is, the girls were supposed to be sleeping, but naturally they were not, in spite of repeated warnings from Beth's mother. "I promised your parents you would get plenty of sleep!" Mrs. Aldrich insisted. "Now, no more talking!"

"I'm glad you didn't go with them," Beth whispered to Anna.

"Me, too," Anna whispered back. "Wild horses couldn't drag me anywhere near the ocean!"

Beth laughed at her friend. "Why are you so scared of the water?"

Anna didn't know the answer to this question. All she knew was that even thinking about going near it frightened her half to death. "I don't know. It's just so cold . . . and creepy, and . . . and . . . I feel like it's out to get me."

Beth giggled. "I'm coming to get you, Anna! Woooooooo!"

Anna laughed, but she shivered, too.

Her parents, who were understanding people and knew how frightened of the sea their daughter was, had not insisted that she accompany them on their own long-held dream: a sailing trip down the coast. Instead, her father had picked her up in his arms and swung her around and said, "Be a good girl, my little palindrome. Fourteen days isn't so terribly long, and then soon it will be your birthday and you will have your very own horse." Anna's mother had hugged her hard and said, "I will miss you so much, Anna— fourteen days will seem like forever to me!"

And although Anna missed them, she was not sorry to miss the ocean trip.

"This is much more fun than sailing!" Beth said, and both girls giggled again. They had smuggled licorice sticks into bed and were already on their twelfth ones as they made plans for the summer, only three weeks away. They'd spend every single day with Anna's horse.

Anna smiled contentedly. "It's going to be so great." Then, looking at her friend anxiously, she added, "You don't feel bad, do you? I mean, that I'll have a horse and you won't?" She hurried on before Beth could answer. "Because I'm thinking H-Rose will be almost as much yours as mine."

Beth handed Anna her thirteenth licorice stick, then took another for herself. "Best friends forever!" she said.

Yes, all was right with Anna's world on Monday.

The terrible news arrived on Tuesday.

The announcement came not as a tornado might, with sudden sound and fury. It arrived more as a cold sea fog, drifting in ominously: a mist of whispers and stricken faces.

The facts were misty, too, except for one: Anna's parents were gone, lost at sea. They would not be coming home. Ever.

Now Anna knew why she had always feared the ocean.

The weather on Tuesday was cold and foggy, and the damp moved right into Anna's heart.

On Wednesday and Thursday adults appeared

and rushed about, making "arrangements" and casting sorrowful looks in Anna's direction.

Quite naturally, the good people of Greeley, New Hampshire—for that is where this story begins—were shocked and saddened.

The whispered concern among neighbors and friends was, of course, What was to become of Anna?

Beth was in favor of Anna's living with her. "Couldn't we adopt her?" she pleaded with her parents.

But Mrs. Aldrich shook her head. "Oh, Beth," she said sadly, "that isn't possible." She paused and then added, "Dad has something to tell you."

Mr. Aldrich looked uncomfortable. "We're moving to Albuquerque, my dear, as soon as school is finished. My job—well, I just received the news . . ."

Beth stared at her parents in disbelief.

"I'm sorry," Mr. Aldrich said. "We *have* to move."

"We were going to tell you yesterday, but . . ." Mrs. Aldrich's voice trailed off.

Beth sobbed and turned to Anna. "It's so unfair!" she cried. "What will you do?"

But Anna, hugging her friend, did not answer, could not answer. Instead, she turned to stare out a rain-streaked window.

Mrs. Aldrich, giving Anna a worried look, said, "It's going to be all right. Anna's aunt Formaldy has been informed of the . . . the circumstances. She has decided to move back to Greeley and take care of her."

Anna, watching a raindrop zigzag down the windowpane, didn't seem to hear.

On Friday there was a memorial service at the church. There were tears and hugs, music and flowers. Everyone felt bad. Everyone was very nice. Everyone said what a shame. "Poor child," they said. "It would be better if she had a good cry. It would be better if she talked." But Anna did not cry, and because there was nothing to say, she did not say anything.

Plenty of people were willing to cry and talk for her, however, and when the memorial service was over, *they* seemed to feel a good deal better.

"Thank goodness her aunt is coming to live with her," they said. "Yes, thank goodness she won't have to go anywhere. At least she'll remain in Familiar Surroundings."

"Yes," they agreed, "there is great solace in being surrounded by familiar objects, old friends. And an aunt."

"But where is she?" Mrs. Aldrich asked. "She's missed the service. She wrote that she would arrive today." Formaldy Farrington rarely came to Greeley these days. It was understood that she was very busy in Chicago doing important things.

Suddenly a figure appeared in the open doorway.

"Ahh, Miss Farrington," cried Mrs. Maplethorpe, "here you are!"

Formaldy Farrington, tall and imposing and as thin as an icicle, paused for a moment and looked around. Her blond hair had been elegantly styled and fell sharply at her chin. Straight bangs framed her narrow face. She wore a finely tailored black suit and black shoes with spiky heels. "You *will* forgive me for my tardiness, won't you?" she said to the room at large, her smile bright.

Mrs. Aldrich stepped forward and said warmly, "I am terribly sorry about your loss."

"My poor, poor brother and his darling little wife," replied Formaldy Farrington. "Yes, it was a severe blow. Quite." A crease formed between her shaped eyebrows. "I feel it deeply. He was, of course, my stepbrother, not really related to me, you know, but I do believe I am the only family he and his wife had." Here she shrugged modestly.

The kind neighbors murmured. "We are all moved by your generosity in taking in Anna," Mrs. McNabb said.

The small crease reappeared on Formaldy Farrington's smooth brow for a moment.

"Oh, yes indeed! My poor orphaned niece," she
exclaimed, raising her chin and looking around her.
"Where is that dear child?" She gazed about the
room, her eyes resting finally on Beth. "Ah, there
you are, you sweet little thing. You do remember
your Aunt Formaldy, don't you?"

Beth flushed and turned to Anna, who was re-
garding her aunt from a distance.

Mrs. Aldrich stepped past Beth, put her arm
around Anna, and brought her forward. "You'll be
amazed to see how much Anna has grown this year,"
she said.

Aunt Formaldy did not seem the least bit embar-
rassed by her mistake. She turned to her niece and
smiled a smile so convincing that the gathered mourn-
ers all found themselves smiling, too. "Of course you
are my own dear niece! And now that you've lost your
mother and father, I will try to take their place."

Anna stared at her aunt and said nothing. Then
she looked away.

"It's been a difficult time for her," said Mrs.
Aldrich.

"But of course it has," Aunt Formaldy assured
her. "We shall have plenty of time to get reac-

quainted, my dear niece and I. I plan to dote on her, you know!" She laughed a pleasant laugh that sounded like tinkling bells. It filled the room and warmed the hearts of all the adults.

The Reverend Robert Simons, who had delivered a moving eulogy, spoke up. "It is good to have you back in our midst, Miss Farrington, even though the circumstances are so difficult."

"Thank you, Reverend," said Formaldy Farrington, holding out a well-manicured hand. Golden bracelets jingled on her wrist. "Yes, I return to the ancestral home."

Although Anna was aware of the fact that ten generations of Farringtons had lived in her house, she had never, not once, heard it referred to as an "ancestral home." That expression made her think of gables and ghosts, drafty rooms and doilies.

True, it was the oldest house in the village of Greeley, and Farringtons had lived there since it was built, in 1749. But it was a warm old house, large, comfortable, and familiar, filled with interesting books and pictures and cozy furniture. Not a bit *ancestral*.

Aunt Formaldy continued, "Yes, no sacrifice for my niece is too great. The Farrington house . . ." She shook her head and sighed. "Improvements will certainly be necessary."

Members of the Historical Society, several of whom were in attendance, greeted this news with quiet delight. "So you intend to make some . . . restorations?" inquired one member delicately.

"Oh, goodness me, yes indeed. Improvements are under way even now, as a matter of fact." Aunt Formaldy flashed her disarming smile. "We shall have to blame those improvements for my inexcusable tardiness today. I have been at the house trying to arrange for them all day!" She hesitated. "I am worried that my niece might be disturbed by the comings and goings of the workers . . . Perhaps she would be more comfortable staying with a friend for a week or two?" She looked around at the assembled townsfolk expectantly.

"Of course!" Mrs. Aldrich exclaimed. "Anna is very welcome in our home until we move."

Beth, who was standing next to Anna, now hugged her hard and said, "I wish it could be forever!"

But Anna had turned to her aunt. Their eyes met, and in that moment Anna realized two things: that Aunt Formaldy was wearing her mother's pearl necklace, and that as bad as things were, they were about to become much worse.

FOG

The week or two that Aunt Formaldy suggested became three weeks, and Anna spent them in the same fog that had descended on her that fateful Tuesday. She got up in the morning and went to bed at night; she dressed when the day started and put on her pajamas when it ended, one day following the next.

Formaldy Farrington did not come to see Anna during these weeks, nor did she telephone. Anna overheard Mrs. Aldrich saying to her husband, "I am sure she is busy. Still, it *is* strange that she doesn't seem more concerned about Anna."

And Anna did not return to her home during that time, not once. She did not even walk past it. The thought of Aunt Formaldy marching through the rooms of her house, finding out about the tree in her backyard . . . well, she just could not bear to think of it.

Beth brought Anna a bag of licorice sticks. But the bag remained unopened on the table next to Anna's bed.

They went to school, but if anyone had asked what had happened in those long last days in class, Anna wouldn't have been able to answer.

In the evening, sitting at the table with the Aldriches, Anna tried to be a good guest. She passed the peas and mashed potatoes; she answered Mr. Aldrich's question "How was school today?" with "Good, thank you." She complimented Beth's little brother on the spaceship he had drawn. But inside, Anna was absent, still stuck in her terrible Tuesday, still lost in her own cold, damp fog.

It was another Tuesday when the Aldrich family took Anna back to her house on Maple Street. In the car, Mrs. Aldrich took Anna's hand in her own, gave it a tight squeeze, and said, "Anna, we are going to miss you! I wish we weren't leaving for Albuquerque tomorrow. But you know, your aunt will take good care of you. I'm sure she wanted to have you back in your own home sooner than this. But as she said, there has been a great deal of work to do . . ." Mrs. Aldrich's voice trailed off as they drove up to the house.

Suddenly Beth gasped. "Look at your house!"

It appeared that the familiar yellow house that Anna loved had died and come back to life as something else—something strange. The twisted apple tree in the front was still there, the rolling lawn still stretched all the way back to the woods, and the large tree in the backyard still towered over the house, but everything else was completely different.

The house was no longer a soft daisy yellow with warm green shutters. It had been painted dead white. The shutters were gone, and heavy curtains masked the windows like closed lids over eyes. And all of the beautiful holly that had surrounded the house had disappeared. In its place were pointed little bushes. A new oval plaque attached to the door said:

FARRINGTON HOUSE
BUILT 1749

As they walked along the path to the front door, Beth put her arm through Anna's and squeezed it.

"Well," said Mrs. Aldrich as she raised the new brass knocker and let it fall.

After a few silent moments, Aunt Formaldy, dressed in a long skirt and silk blouse, opened the door, her face wreathed in smiles for the Aldriches.

"How delightful! Do come in," she said, fingering the pearl necklace. "You simply must see the improvements I've made."

Anna stared past Aunt Formaldy. Instead of the familiar jumble of raincoats and jackets hanging on wooden pegs that she had last seen in the large hallway, there were two ornate mirrors reflecting new rose-covered wallpaper. Uncomfortable-looking chairs were lined up on one side of the hall. A large grandfather clock ticked loudly on the other side. The curving staircase was now covered in a richly patterned Persian carpet.

"Come in, come in!" said Aunt Formaldy. "I think you will find that I have given Farrington House a much more *authentic* style," she murmured to Mrs. Aldrich as she took her by the arm and steered her through the hallway and up the newly carpeted stairs.

Anna followed silently. What had happened to her comfortable old home? She clenched her hands into tight little balls as her aunt said, "First things first!" and then opened the door to Anna's bedroom.

Beth, who had said nothing since entering the house, whispered, "Anna! Your room!"

Anna's bedroom had been transformed. It was now a girl's room from the nineteenth century, complete with ancient toys, yellowed schoolbooks, and an old dollhouse. An antique porcelain doll dressed in blue satin was propped up on a velvet-covered rocking chair.

"Oh, my!" said Mrs. Aldrich, her eyes wide. She glanced at Anna in alarm.

Aunt Formaldy smiled. "Nothing is too good for my niece."

Anna was not smiling, however. She was looking around for her collection of horses. They seemed to have vanished, along with her own dolls and the stuffed animals she hadn't played with for ages but still loved. What had become of them? As she gazed at her room and at the odd assortment of old-fashioned toys, she had to bite her tongue to keep from crying out.

"And now for the rest of the house!" announced Aunt Formaldy. "Just a quick tour, I'm sorry to say, because I have an important meeting with the Historical Society in a few minutes." She locked her arm through Mrs. Aldrich's and led her through the rest of the rooms, Anna and Beth trailing behind.

Anna's parents' room was now Aunt Formaldy's. Every single trace of Anna's mother and father was gone. Instead, the room was filled with chairs covered in brocade and an enormous canopied bed draped in satin. "It was difficult to decide which was the best room," Aunt Formaldy purred. "But this will do."

Anna's mother's office had become a "sitting room." Antique chairs and little mahogany tables had taken the place of the old desk and the computer, the well-thumbed dictionary, and the thesaurus. The big soft chair Anna had curled up in with her mother for stories was gone.

Gone, gone, gone. Everything good about Anna's house was gone. And in its place was everything bad. Especially Aunt Formaldy.

A CHARMING
ROOM

Yes, goodbye, do keep in touch," Aunt Formaldy said at the door when the tour was over. "And do not worry—we shall be very cozy, the two of us." She looked down at Anna and added, "My niece is going to be just fine."

I will never ever be fine, thought Anna. *Not ever.*

Anna walked outside with the Aldriches. Beth burst into tears as she hugged her friend goodbye, but although Anna's eyes grew misty, she didn't cry. She had not cried once since that terrible Tuesday. She waved goodbye to the departing car, took a deep breath, and turned back to the cold white house. Her aunt was nowhere to be seen.

Sighing deeply, she climbed the stairs. The newly polished banister curved elegantly upward and the thick carpeting muffled her footsteps. Framed photographs of stern ancestors gazed indifferently at her from the walls. Anna went into her strange room, closed the door, and frowned at her bed. So many satin and lace pillows had been arranged at the head of the bed that there was scarcely room for her, but she pushed some aside and lay down. She squeezed her eyes tight and took great gulps of air.

"My dear child, whatever are you doing on that bed?" Aunt Formaldy was staring down at Anna. "For goodness' sake, look what you've done—you have disarranged everything."

Anna looked up at her aunt, surprised, but jumped off the bed when she saw her aunt's eyes sharpen into little pinpricks.

"But this is my bed . . ." Anna began.

"Oh my, no," Aunt Formaldy said with a laugh, as if Anna had just made a very good joke. "Whatever can you be thinking?"

Anna blinked.

"This is not your room," Aunt Formaldy said. She spoke as if Anna were quite out of her mind.

"Where is my room then?" Anna frowned, thinking of the ornate rooms she had visited.

"You shall see! A charming room—I am sure you will be quite comfortable there, although I could certainly have used it for something else."

The charming room, it turned out, was the old sewing room. In truth, it was more like a closet than a room. Anna's mother had kept her sewing machine here. But the bolts of fabric and the boxes of buttons and needles and thread, along with the sewing machine, were gone now. In their place were an iron bed, an old chest of drawers, and a rickety table with a lamp. Although there was a surprisingly large window for such a little place, the room was gloomy.

"I expect you to be quite comfortable here," said Aunt Formaldy, speaking from the hallway. The door barely opened wide enough for even Anna to squeeze in, so her aunt had remained outside. "And since this room will not be part of my house tours for the Historical Society, I ask you to keep this door closed at all times."

And with those words Aunt Formaldy pulled the door shut.

THE JUSTIN CASE TREE

Anna stood in the small space between her bed and the chest of drawers and waited impatiently for the sound of her aunt's steps to fade away. The sewing room was not by any means as nice or as large as Anna's own room.

But would Aunt Formaldy have given it to her if she had known what was right outside the window? Anna caught her breath—would she find *that* changed and ruined, too? Hardly daring to hope, she pushed aside the thin curtain and pulled up the sash. Then, with a glance at the closed door, she stepped through the window and into the branches of a great tree.

"Ahhhh," she sighed, looking all around her.

At least here, in this one place, everything was exactly as it had been. The pear-shaped green leaves made their whispery sound as always, a gentle rustling lullaby. Sunlight and shade chased each other up and down the trunk. The branches, broad and strong and spreading almost straight out from the trunk, seemed to welcome her, and for a moment Anna could imagine that everything was as it always had been—that her mother and father might at any moment join her here with mugs of chocolate and a plate of cookies. They would sit on the little yellow sofa securely nestled between the tree's branches, or in the pale green rocking chairs next to it. Then they would dip their cookies in sweet hot cocoa and play board games until bedtime.

For this was a very special tree.

Of course everyone in Greeley knew of the tree. It was such a famous tree that it had a name: the Justin Case tree. No one knew what kind of tree it was, or who Mr. Case had been. Anna's father had told her that her great-, great-, many times great-grandmother, Lucinda Anna Farrington, had planted it back when the house was new. He called the acorns "nutberries," but when she asked him why, all he could say was that was what his father had called them.

Yes, everyone knew the tree from the outside. But hardly anyone knew about the *inside*.

Not even Aunt Formaldy.

No one knew that the tree was filled with snug corners and cozy nooks furnished with chairs and tables. People would have been very surprised indeed to see the stairway leading up to comfy cushions and bookshelves filled with books and games, and up farther to a secret spot where a hammock swung gently among the leaves, and up still farther to the very top, where there was a lookout post. Anyone standing up there could see the whole neighborhood and a good part of the village of Greeley but still remain invisible.

Anna and her parents had sometimes eaten here in the tree by candlelight, at a low table covered with a green cloth and surrounded by pillows. The leaves were so thick that even though the sun could slip through and bathe everything in a soft green glow during the day, at night no one could see the candlelight flickering on the tables or the twinkly electric lights suspended from the branches.

Anna gazed at this secret hideaway, and the shadow of a very small smile flitted across her face for a second. What would Aunt Formaldy think if she knew Anna had ended up with the best room in the house?

HOW KIND
OF YOU

On Saturday the phone rang. Anna went to answer it, but Aunt Formaldy stepped in front of her and said in an icy voice, "When the phone rings, I shall answer it. If I am not here, no one will answer it." She cleared her throat, picked up the receiver, and said in her tinkly-bells voice, "This is the Formaldy Farrington residence, Formaldy Farrington speaking. Who? Oh! How kind of you to call, Mrs. Aldrich . . . Well, she is doing as well as can be expected, poor child. I have scarcely left her side, and we get along like two peas in a pod . . . No need to worry about her—she is busy and happy and well looked after! . . . No, she's off with friends, but I will indeed tell her you called."

Anna stared at her aunt in amazement. She was lying!

Suddenly Anna realized that everything about Aunt Formaldy was a lie. And no one seemed to know it but her.

Strange as it may seem, the thought that Aunt Formaldy lied about everything appealed to Anna. *Maybe other grownups had lied, too—maybe they had lied about what had happened to her parents!* Maybe they had changed their minds at the last minute and hadn't gone on a sailing trip, after all. Maybe they had gone on a car trip instead and had simply become lost. On TV shows people were always showing up after recovering from amnesia. Could both her parents get amnesia at the same time?

From that moment on, Anna started to practice thinking this way. It was far better than thinking that her parents were gone for good. Maybe one day soon they would just walk in the front door and say, "We're so glad to be home at last! We couldn't call because we were in the hospital, but now we're perfectly fine and everything is going to be just the way it was before."

Whenever the truth came too close, whenever the unbearable thought tried to enter her head that her parents were never, ever coming back, she would concentrate on saying the alphabet backward. "ZYX-WVUTSRQPONMLKJIHGFEDCBA!" she'd recite to herself, until the bad thoughts slunk off into their dark corners.

The summer days passed, one after another. The phone rang often, but no longer for Anna. There were comings and goings, but Anna saw no one. The ladies from the Historical Society came frequently, and Anna often overheard them exclaiming over Aunt Formaldy's antiques and the authentic restorations she had made. Anna's mother used to call them the Hysterical Society because they got so upset about modern doorknobs and plastic fences.

Apart from making trips to the library, Anna stayed in her tree and read. She read adventure books and mysteries, and especially books about horses. School would not start again for several weeks, and Anna did not know whether she dreaded it or looked forward to it. It would be a new, big school with many strangers. But maybe she would find a friend. She knew no one could ever replace Beth, but she longed for someone to talk to.

As for the terrible event that had changed Anna's life forever, Aunt Formaldy made only one reference. "A silly thing to do, sailing off on a boat like that," she had sniffed, shaking her head in disgust. "Your father was terribly impractical, young woman. Yes, and your mother, too. Imagine! Their ship lost at sea! Your father was always losing things as a boy."

And so it was that Anna went from being a happy, loved child to being a sad, forgotten child, all in the twinkling of an eye. Yes, she still lived in the house she had grown up in, but now it seemed a stranger's house. And yes, the house still sat on the corner of Maple and Cross streets in the New Hampshire village of Greeley, but to Anna it felt as if the whole property had been transported to a town she had never even visited, perhaps Tallahassee or Sheboygan.

PICTURES? OF WHOM?

Sometimes at night before she fell asleep, Anna would try to remember what her parents looked like—her mother's flaming red hair and laughing eyes, her father's wide friendly smile.

But the memory of her parents' faces was fading. This frightened her. In her dreams, though, Anna could see her parents clearly, and she could hear them speak. Her father would say, "Let's build a paddock for your horse today," and smile his huge smile. Her mother appeared in her dreams, too, holding Anna on her lap and saying, "Everything is going to be all right," and sometimes she would sing to her the old song: *"What'll I do-o-o-o when yo-ou-ou are f-a-a-ar away?"*

Anna would wake up still hearing her mother's sweet voice, and she would try to hold on to the pic-

ture of the loving eyes and the warm embrace. Then
it would all fade away, like steam on the bathroom
mirror.

The more Anna worried about forgetting her parents' faces, the more she could not remember them.
One day she approached Aunt Formaldy. "Where
are the pictures of my parents?" she asked.

Aunt Formaldy was leafing through a decorating
magazine and had to be asked the question several
times before she turned her attention, such as it was,
to Anna. "Pictures?" she said. Her flat eyes regarded
Anna with suspicion. "Of whom?"

"Of my parents," Anna repeated bravely. It was
rare that she said the word "parents" out loud.

"Well, I certainly don't know," Aunt Formaldy
replied. "Perhaps they ended up at the landfill." She
wrinkled her nose. "Along with everything else."

Anna felt a stab of pain. The pictures and the piano and the books and her mother's little boxes—
were they all at the dump, buried under orange peels
and meat scraps, eggshells and coffee grounds and
worse?

Was nothing left of her parents' belongings, nothing left of her life with them? Maybe none of it had
ever happened. Maybe they had never really existed.
Maybe she had always been alone and afraid.

Aunt Formaldy looked at Anna in irritation and said, "My guests will be arriving shortly—you will want to stay in your room."

As Anna passed through the hallway on her way upstairs, she caught a glimpse of herself in one of the large gold-plated mirrors. Staring out at her was a new Anna, pale and plain and sullen-looking. Not much to recommend her, as she overheard her aunt say one day. The old Anna had had a bright face with shining blue eyes and little freckles across her nose. The freckles and blue eyes were from her mother. The old Anna had had a great big smile that lit up an entire room. That was from her father.

The new Anna made a face, stuck out her tongue at her reflection, went upstairs, stepped through the window in her room, and threw herself onto the yellow sofa in her tree. She did not cry. Instead, she lay very, very still, her eyes closed. If anyone had seen her, they might have thought she had fallen asleep.

Inside, however, she was yelling and screaming and throwing things. "You stupid, wicked lady! You . . . you *turnip*!" In her mind, she grabbed the doilies and tore them into shreds and threw the antique candlesticks at the ugly mirrors in the hallway. "I HATE you!"

At last she sighed and took out her notebook. It

said "Anna's Book of Lists" on the cover. Turning to a new page, she wrote, "*Aunt Formaldy and the Bad Things That Will Happen to Her*" at the top.

> *1. A poisonous snake will get into her bed and bite her.*
> *2. She will be arrested and taken to jail in handcuffs.*
> *3. When she takes off her hat, all her hair will fall out.*
> *4. Fire ants will get into her clothes.*
> *5. Mom and Dad will come back and throw her out.*

She would add one a day, she thought.

She leafed through her book of lists. Favorite movies, favorite books, the names of all the horses she had ever ridden, the names of all the states she had visited. Anna made lists of everything.

The first list Anna had ever written looked like this:

Wat I Want for Crismas

1. a hrose
2.

3.
4.
5.
6.
7.
8.
9.
10.
That is oll I can think of
Signed, Anna Farrington, age 6

She and her mother used to smile whenever they looked back at that old list, and "h-rose" became their own little joke.

Anna did not get a horse that year, since she was only six. But when she turned ten, she got riding lessons so that when she finally turned eleven, she would be ready for her very own horse at last.

In preparation for that great day, Anna and her mother had spent hours fixing up the stall in the barn. They sanded the walls. They swept and scrubbed the floor. They brought in fresh straw. Anna had made a sign for the door. "H-Rose," it said. But all that was in the past. In Anna's other life.

When Anna dared to mention to Aunt Formaldy that she was to have had a horse for her eleventh birthday, Aunt Formaldy's response was simple. "No birthday, no horses," she said. "Goodness me, no." And that was that. After that, Anna tried not to think about the horse stall again. In fact, she had not even been back there since the day her parents kissed her goodbye.

Anna added #6 to her Aunt Formaldy list:

> 6. I will get a horse no matter what Aunt Formaldy says.

But that seemed even less likely than the poisonous snake. She sighed and closed her book of lists. Then she took out a piece of paper and a pen.

> Dear Beth,
> Do you have poisonous snakes in Albuquerque? Just wondering.
> Aunt Formaldy is terrible. She is a fake, and a fraud and a phony.
> Maybe things will be better when school starts. I wonder what middle school will be like? It's so big!

She did not finish her letter. But she felt a little better, and it wasn't long before she picked up her current book. She was reading *Misty of Chincoteague* for the third time. At least she could read undisturbed for days on end.

PART 2

GERMS

Three stories tall and as big as a football field, Greeley Expanded Regional Middle School—called "GERMS" by all the students—was even larger and more intimidating than Anna had imagined. Children from eight different towns attended GERMS. She watched as swarms of chatting students, greeting each other with waves and backslaps, streamed through a large doorway at the left end of the building. Anna looked around for a familiar face but couldn't find one, so she walked up the steps to the big door and entered by herself. Inside, students walked purposefully down long corridors, glancing at official-looking papers they held in their hands. Anna didn't have any papers. No one had given them to her. Class was supposed to begin in three minutes and she had no idea where to go.

The office was on the first floor. A woman behind the reception desk looked weary and rested her head in her hand as she spoke. "Are you lost?" she asked, flipping through papers and reaching for the pencil behind her ear. A loud bell rang and doors slammed.

Anna nodded.

The woman smiled at her. "I think we can figure that out. Didn't you receive your papers in the mail?"

"I don't think so," said Anna, wondering what her aunt had done with them.

"Well, never mind. We'll see what we can do." But the phone buzzed again and then three people interrupted with urgent messages.

Finally Anna was on her way to Room 322. She hurried down an empty hallway and up two flights of stairs. To the right and down another hall. Room 344, 346, 348—she was going the wrong way. Anna stopped and looked at the number again. It must be on the other side of the building, she thought in dismay. She was going to be very late.

Anna's footsteps sounded loud on the linoleum floor. She glanced down at her feet and stopped short, staring at her socks. The left one was blue. The right one was red. Her room had been dark when she dressed, but had she really done something so stupid, and on the first day of school?

"Are you lost?"

A tall man with glasses and a mustache frowned down at her and then at the paper with her room number. He was wearing a nametag that said "Principal."

"I'm looking for Room 322."

"I'm headed that way. Follow me," he said briskly, already striding down the hall. "We try not to be late here," he added over his shoulder.

Anna hurried after him. By the time she reached Room 322 she was panting. "Here you go," said the principal as he opened the door.

Anna looked inside. Everyone was seated. Breathing heavily, with little prickles of sweat on her forehead, she mumbled, "Sorry."

Twenty pairs of eyes stared at Anna's face.

Twenty pairs of eyes slid down to Anna's socks. Someone snickered.

Anna wished with all her might that she would burst into flames.

Instead of bursting into flames, however, she sat down in the only empty seat left. The bottom of one of the legs was missing, so the desk rocked back and forth and made a loud clacking sound when she moved so much as a finger. The boy in front of her let out a loud laugh.

"You must be Anna," said a pleasant plump woman.

"Yes," replied Anna, trying to keep her desk from rocking back and forth. She was mortified to hear her voice squeak.

"Welcome to middle school, Anna. My name is Ms. Pritz, and I am your core curriculum teacher." She looked over her glasses at the children. "Now, I know most of you from elementary last year— isn't it nice that we have all moved on together?" Ms. Pritz smiled. "We have some new faces, though, haven't we? Let's see," she said, glancing down at her papers, "which one of you is Bertha Sampedro?"

The boy in front, who had turned completely around in his chair to stare, let out a snort, and the rest of the class giggled.

"I am," the girl next to Anna said in a quiet voice. Anna took a peek at her out of the corner of her eye. She was very pretty, with masses of dark curls framing a pale face, but the most interesting thing about her was her coat. At least Anna thought it was a coat, or maybe a big shirt. It was bright red and long, with big pockets and large white buttons. "That is my given name, but—"

The boy interrupted with a howl of laughter.

"Someone *gave* you that name? Some gift." The rest of the class tittered.

"Walker, please," objected Ms. Pritz wearily. She turned back to the dark-haired girl. "Welcome, Bertha. I am sure you will enjoy being in our class." Bertha swept her eyes over the other students but said nothing.

"Let's see, we have already met Anna . . ." Ms. Pritz went on, shuffling some papers.

"I think 'Sock Girl' suits her better," hissed the boy called Walker as he turned to face Anna. Walker's face was round, almost pudgy, but the rest of him was skinny. He looked tall for his age. He might have been a nice-looking boy, thought Anna, except for the meanness in his cold eyes.

Ms. Pritz studied the paper in front of her for a moment. "It's a shame your parents didn't show up for our informational meeting last week, Anna. Perhaps you could tell them that we strongly encourage parental involvement in this class." Ms. Pritz looked up from her sheet to smile at Anna.

"Um." Anna's face turned beet red. "They . . . they're . . . they can't come to meetings. They're . . . on vacation." She stopped in confusion.

Twenty faces turned to look at her, but only

Ms. Pritz said anything. "Well, we'll get everything straightened out, I'm sure."

Anna felt her throat tighten, as if an invisible hand were squeezing it.

No one can straighten anything out, she thought to herself. *No one.*

NEW
SOCKS?

On Monday Anna left for school early so she could be sure not to be late. Most of the students were already there, talking and laughing. Anna hurried quickly to her seat. She could hear Walker clear across the room.

"So what's with the hair, Joshy boy? Looks like you got electrocuted," he said as Josh sat down.

"Ha ha," said Josh, quickly running his hand over his head.

Walker spotted a girl called Allison. "Wearing your mom's shirt today, Ally baby?"

Walker looked around restlessly. At that moment the new girl, Bertha, walked in. Her hands were deep in the pockets of her long, floppy coat. Giving the students a cool look, she glided to her seat.

"She's so stuck-up," muttered one of the girls behind Anna.

"I know," agreed another. "And look at that thing she's wearing. She thinks she's so cool." Both girls laughed loudly.

Anna studied Bertha out of the corner of her eye. The girl's eyes were half closed, as if she were not very interested in the people around her. She *does* look conceited, Anna thought.

Walker strolled over. "Beulah, hey, Beee-ulah," he said in a singsongy voice. "Isn't that your name? Or is it Gertrude? I forget." Bertha gave him a brief, dismissive look, as if he were a fly buzzing around the room.

Ms. Pritz had not arrived yet, and Anna sat in her chair hoping Walker would bypass her. No such luck.

"New socks, Sock Girl?" he said, giving up on Bertha and fixing on Anna. Anna glanced at her feet without thinking and felt her face turn bright red, all the way up to the roots of her hair. Walker snorted loudly at his success while a few of the others giggled.

"Good morning, class," said Ms. Pritz, walking in and closing the door. Anna breathed a sigh of relief.

The rest of the week was no better. Each morning Anna sat down alone while the other students chatted and giggled before Ms. Pritz arrived, and Walker roamed the room making comments. Anna had hoped that she and Bertha would be friends, since they were the only new students in the class. But Bertha remained standoffish. Once Anna smiled at her, but the quiet girl had already turned away. And once Bertha picked up Anna's pencil from the floor and handed it to her. When Anna thanked her, Bertha nodded but didn't say anything.

It was going to be a very long school year.

"Today we're going to the library," Ms. Pritz announced one morning. "And I want each of you to choose a book to read. We will have book reports at the end of next week." The class groaned.

"But that's only like ten days!" cried Jennifer.

"Reading is dumb," Walker stated.

Anna sighed. Was she the only one in the class who liked to read?

She glanced at Bertha, who was wearing a lime green vest today over an orange shirt. Her pale face was expressionless.

Suddenly Bertha turned to look straight at Anna and—there was no mistaking it—crossed her eyes.

A laugh unexpectedly bubbled up in Anna's throat. In surprise she tried to stop it, which started a coughing fit, which brought tears to her eyes and turned her face bright red again. Ms. Pritz turned around and said, "Perhaps you would like to excuse yourself and get a drink of water, Anna."

When Anna returned, she found a note on her desk. It said, "My favorite book is *The Mystery of the Lost Horses*. What's yours?"

BELA BLOWS BIG

When Anna got to school the next day, Bertha was already sitting at her desk next to Anna's. She was wearing the floppy red coat again.

"My name isn't actually Bertha," she said suddenly, in a voice so soft that Anna wasn't sure she had actually heard it.

Anna smiled tentatively. "It's not?"

"It is, but it's pronounced *Bear*-ta," she replied, speaking a bit louder. "Besides, everyone who knows me calls me Sam." She paused. A dark curl slipped over her eye, and she brushed it back with her hand.

"I'm Anna," said Anna, not knowing what else to say. She was out of practice talking to people.

"I'm glad to meet you," said Sam politely.

"Me, too," replied Anna, kicking herself for sounding so stupid. Maybe she's not that stuck-up, thought Anna. She was about to say something else, but the door opened and Ms. Pritz came in, looking excited.

"I suppose you have all heard from your parents about the approaching hurricane," she said.

Hurricane! Anna had heard nothing about it. There was no one to hear anything from at home. She listened uneasily to her classmates, who all began talking at once.

"I hope we lose power," Erin said, "and they have to close the schools."

"A hurricane this far north! That's weird," said Noah.

"It's because of global warming," Amy said.

"There's no such thing as global warming," Walker announced.

Ms. Pritz brought the class to order. "We have a lot of work to do today. I have the feeling school will be canceled for the next few days."

After school Anna looked for Sam, but she had already left. Anna wondered where she lived.

On her way home Anna stopped at the library and went directly to the newspaper section. The headlines were larger than usual.

The New York Times said:

Hurricane Threatens East Coast

The *Boston Herald* screamed:

Big Bela Barrels Bostonward!

The Boston Globe, which was the big newspaper for the entire region, including New Hampshire, had a front-page article:

BOSTON BRACES FOR BELA

The National Weather Service issued a warning for the entire East Coast as Bela, a category 4 hurricane, gathered strength off the Virginia coast. Bela, with sustained winds of more than 140 miles an hour, is expected to reach as far north as New Hampshire and Maine, bringing the threat of widespread damage, including flooding, the downing of trees and power lines . . .

Anna dropped the paper and ran home as fast as she could. *Downing of trees, downing of trees*—the words rang in her head over and over until they sounded like nonsense syllables.

She hurried to the backyard and stood beneath her tree, looking up anxiously into the branches and wondering what she should be looking for. Were any of the branches cracked? Could they just break off, bringing the yellow sofa and the tables and chairs with them? Would the whole tree be uprooted?

She wondered if there was someone she should call.

She looked at her house. It seemed to stare back at her, cold and unfriendly. If she had to make a choice between the house and her tree, she thought, she would choose the tree. No question about it. Her tree was her real home. If the hurricane came and blew the stupid old house to Timbuktu, Anna wouldn't care. Not now. Not one bit!

It could even take the barn with it, she thought. She glanced over at it now and wondered if the horse stall still looked the same as that day she and her mother had put the finishing touches on it. She wondered if she would ever be able to enter it again. "ZYXWVU . . . ," she started, pushing the memory away from her.

Anna walked to the fence at the back of the yard. She could just see the Claiborne house through the trees on the other side of a large backyard. Old Mrs. Claiborne had been such a nice lady, she thought. But she had died a year ago, and now the house was for sale. No help there. No help anywhere. Anna was all alone.

WIDESPREAD UPROOTING OF TREES

It was the smell that woke her up early the next morning—a dark, heavy smell. Like the zoo, Anna thought. She lay in bed, half awake, thinking of lions and tigers. It was quiet. Too quiet, she realized suddenly, and she sat up. Where were the chattering sparrows? She strained her ears: no wind, no rustling of leaves, no birdsong or cars swooshing by, no dogs barking. What was happening?

Then she remembered the hurricane. She jumped out of bed, ran to the window, and hurried out into the tree. The tree was silent, more silent than she had ever known. "What's happening?" she said out loud. She felt breathless and inhaled deeply. The air was thick and hard to breathe. It smelled foreign, as if it had slid over Greeley from some faraway place.

She climbed the stairs to the lookout at the top of

the tree, parted the leaves, and peered out. "How strange," she said. A heavy yellow mist had settled over the village like a veil. She could scarcely see across the empty street.

Something serious was about to happen. Where was everybody?

"Ooooow! Oooooooooooooow!" It was Jasper, Mr. Osgood's little poodle from down the street, howling at the top of his lungs. He sounded terrified, and Anna felt prickles on the back of her neck. A flock of crows rose up suddenly from a nearby tree, screeching and cawing.

Anna remembered her radio, on the shelf in the tree with all the games, and hurried to turn it on. The radio announcer's voice was tense.

"Bela is a big one, that's for sure. We haven't seen a hurricane of this magnitude come this far north in over one hundred years. The governors of Massachusetts and New Hampshire have declared a state of emergency. All schools in both states have been closed. Damaging winds and as much as ten inches of rain are possible when the storm hits the Boston area this morning. The National Weather Service predicts massive power outages caused by the widespread uprooting of trees . . ."

Widespread uprooting of trees!

The strange wet smell filled the air like the dank, dark smell of lurking wild things.

Where was Aunt Formaldy? Anna went back inside, hurried downstairs with her radio, and looked around. No one was there.

Maybe Aunt Formaldy was waiting out the storm with friends. Anna pictured the other children from her class, safe and sound with their parents, as she had been with her own parents during thunderstorms. Once they had lost power and had to use flashlights and candles. Anna had thought it was fun.

But now she was alone, listening to the radio, and it wasn't fun. *Widespread damage, flooding, downed trees . . . Please don't be blown down*, she thought desperately. *Please, please, please don't.*

"The leading edge of the hurricane is now just south of Boston and moving rapidly northward. This monster storm is still packing winds of over 120 miles an hour, and we strongly urge all residents of Massachusetts and New Hampshire to take cover immediately."

Anna felt her ears pop, as if she had just ridden down Jake's Hill fast on her bike. Her neighbor's dog, Jasper, continued to howl. The radio started crackling, and Anna turned it off. She noticed that her hands were shaking.

She sat down at the table in the kitchen. Then she stood up. She sat down again. The door to the dining room slammed shut.

"Aunt Formaldy?" said Anna. But there was no answer. "I'm scared," she whispered to no one.

Then she heard a new sound. At first she thought a train was approaching from a long way away. It got closer and closer, and just as she thought, *There are no trains around here*, WHAAP! A blast of wind slammed into the house so hard that the old structure shuddered from top to bottom. Anna heard something crash, but was it inside or outside? She ran into the living room. Everything seemed in order. She pulled aside the curtain to look outside.

Anna blinked. Nothing seemed to be on the ground—everything had been tossed up and was whirling about: flying leaves and sticks and papers and dirt, even patio chairs. The other side of the street appeared far away, as though she were looking from the wrong end of a telescope. In the distance, through the strange yellow air, she could see trees waving wildly, their branches caught up in a furious frenzy.

The wind roared. Anna watched as a garbage can barreled down the street silently, its crashing muted by the furious blast. A shutter detached itself from a faraway house and smashed into the window of a car parked out front. Anna covered her ears, but that did not block out the pounding of the wind on the house. The old house groaned and creaked. Would the hurricane knock it down with her in it? It might. She had seen pictures in newspapers.

CRAAACK! Anna watched the old oak tree across the street crash heavily onto a parked car. The lights flickered.

"My tree!" she screamed. She bounded upstairs, swept aside the curtain, and peered out the window. The odd pear-shaped leaves were waving about wildly, but the tree was still standing.

CRAAAACK! Anna ran downstairs, and another tree was lying across the street. It was a pine tree, one of the large ancient ones that had been standing for at least a hundred years. Then the lights flickered again and went out.

It was dark now. Not pitch black, like night, but a different kind of dark, so strange because it was still morning. Anna stared out the window. The world whirled, a jumble of knocked-down trees and debris. A pair of Rollerblades sped down the middle of the street as if worn by a ghost.

Then the rain started. As though a colossal faucet had been turned on up in the sky, the water fell not in drops but in bucketfuls.

Over the noise Anna thought she could hear a siren. She closed her eyes.

CRRAAAAAAA-AAAACK!

This time the sound was so loud, so close, that Anna knew it must be her tree.

A dull, sad feeling coiled around her, squeezing her breath out. For a whole minute she stood frozen, too afraid to look, barely breathing.

If the tree is gone, she thought, *so am I*.

At last, with shaking knees, she made her way upstairs again. She fumbled for her flashlight and shone it into the darkness outside her window, expecting the worst.

But her tree was still standing, tall and broad and silent. In fact, in the midst of the howling wind and the rain, it appeared almost serene, as if the hurricane were happening someplace else.

"Oh, tree," she murmured.

Anna opened the window and stepped out. Her eyes grew wide as she looked around her.

Outside, the wind still moaned and the rain still hammered against the roof of the house, but here, inside the tree, it was calm.

Everything was as she had left it: her half-finished cookie, her collection of lists, the book she was reading—all dry as a bone. She ran up the stairs to the lookout and parted the dense leaves for a moment so that she could peek out. The wind howled and a torrent of water hit her in the face.

How can this be? Anna wondered, quickly letting the leaves protect her again. She climbed down to the yellow sofa nestled securely in the branches and sat very still, listening. She could barely hear the sounds of the hurricane from here.

The rain drummed on the roof of the house, but from where she sat it sounded like a gentle shower. The wind whipped through other trees, but here inside her own tree it was still. Every now and then she could hear a fire truck or an ambulance in the distance, but that was all.

At last it was night. Anna lit a candle, climbed to her lookout, and parted the leaves. The streetlights were out and all the houses in the neighborhood were dark. The wind still moaned through the trees, but the rain had almost stopped.

Anna went back to the yellow sofa and pulled up the small comforter that lay at one end. She blew out the candle, snuggled in, and closed her eyes. The soft lullaby of the leaves soothed her and the gentle warmth of the branches embraced her, and she fell asleep.

All through the night the wind blew. But Anna slept on, never dreaming of what the wind was carrying with it.

NO ONE
TO TELL

My dear, what a storm! Are you all right? I
was quite beside myself last night worrying about
you."

For a moment Anna, sitting in the kitchen eating
cereal, thought Aunt Formaldy was speaking to
her from the living room. "I'm fine," she began,
surprised by her aunt's sudden concern, but Aunt
Formaldy was already continuing.

"No, no, everything is quite all right here, thank
you, although we have a terrible mess in the backyard . . . Yes, branches and leaves and . . ." Anna realized that her aunt was on the phone. "No, no, I
stayed at the inn yesterday—no point in risking having that tree fall on me! . . . Who? Oh. Of course.
My darling niece and I both enjoyed the inn—so
comfortable, you know, quite authentic."

Anna practically choked on a raisin. Did anyone at all realize what a fraud her aunt was?

"Oh really?" Aunt Formaldy continued. "How charming. Yes, of course, I am happy to speak to him about our tree . . . Good morning to you, Mr. Cincinnati. Your wife says you would like to photograph me with our funny old tree for your newspaper . . . Oh, my, yes. Well, Farrington trees cannot be knocked down that easily! I expect it will stand for another two hundred years." She laughed gaily. "No, no, I am happy to make myself available. Anytime. Yes, you too, very nice to speak with you."

Anna heard her aunt hang up the phone. She hoped she would not come into the kitchen. But she did. "Oh," her aunt said, scowling at Anna as if trying to remember just who this strange girl was. "Well, it's good you are here. I would like you to clean up the backyard this morning. I have never seen such a mess." Then she turned and left.

Anna washed her cereal bowl and put it away, reviewing in her mind the list of "Bad Things That Will Happen to Aunt Formaldy." She thought of a new one:

7. The next time there's a storm, Aunt Formaldy will be blown away.

This morning when she had awakened, Anna had been surprised to find herself in the tree, curled up on the yellow sofa, her radio still in her hand. And then it had all come back to her—the wind, the rain, and the chaos outside. But most of all, the peculiar stillness she had discovered inside the branches of her tree.

She sighed. There was no one to tell, no one to share this discovery with.

She missed her friend Beth, she missed her old life. Most of all, she missed her parents.

THE BARN

School was canceled again while work crews cleared the streets and the power company fixed the lights. Anna had planned on walking around the village to see all the damage. Now she would have to spend the whole day trying to clean up the mess. Aunt Formaldy's word was law in Anna's new world.

Anna looked at the backyard. It would take her forever to pick up all the tree limbs and leaves and trash that carpeted the lawn. "Aunt Formaldy," she muttered, "I wish you would fall off a cliff."

She wandered over to a large dead branch and tried to lift one end. It was too heavy, and it slipped out of her hands. Then suddenly she heard a voice.

"Need help with that?"

Anna looked up. It was Sam.

"Sam!" she exclaimed. "What're you doing here?"

"I'm exploring my new neighborhood." Sam smiled shyly.

"Your neighborhood?" repeated Anna, not understanding. "Where do you live?"

Sam pointed through the thick trees at the old Claiborne house in the distance. "There."

A funny feeling came over Anna. "We're neighbors?"

Sam shrugged and took her hands out of the deep pockets of her red coat. "Seems so." She smiled and pulled at the large branch. "I'll take this end."

"Thanks," said Anna, flushing with pleasure. Grabbing the other end, she suddenly noticed that it was a beautiful day. The air was clear and dry and smelled like fall leaves. A soft breeze rippled over the grass, and a robin caroled in a tree.

Sam didn't say anything as they dragged branches to the edge of the woods. And Anna, out of practice at having conversations, was silent, too.

Finally Sam asked, "Do you usually get storms like the one yesterday?"

"No," said Anna. "Not like that." She paused and then hurried on. "I was scared that my . . . about a tree falling on my house."

Sam gazed up at the Justin Case tree. "You mean

this one. It *is* pretty big," she agreed. She walked around it, considering. "It would make a good tree house."

"Yes," said Anna, suddenly cautious, "it would."

Sam stared up into the tree for a moment more, then turned away. She picked up another stick. "Have you always lived here?" she asked after a while.

Anna nodded. "All my life. How about you? Where are you from?"

"Nowhere. Everywhere."

Anna waited for her to explain, but she didn't.

"Where'd you live before this?" Anna finally asked.

"Switzerland. And before that France. And before that England."

"Really?" said Anna. She wished she could say something interesting, like "Oh, I've been to Switzerland—it's beautiful." But she had never been out of the United States, and to be perfectly honest, she wasn't exactly sure where Switzerland was.

"I'm here in New Hampshire because my parents think I'm forgetting how to be American," Sam said, sighing ever so slightly. "They don't come to New Hampshire very often themselves."

"They don't live here with you?" asked Anna.

"On weekends. Or they *will* be, but so far they've been too busy in Washington to make it up here." She gave a little self-conscious laugh. "Parents," she said. "Who needs them anyway?"

Anna quickly bent down to tie her shoe, and Sam said in a stricken voice, "I'm sorry, I didn't mean that. Gosh." She paused. "Mrs. Birkenhead told me about your parents."

Anna stared at her shoelace. Left loop . . . around . . . right loop . . . pull. She took a deep breath. ZYXWVUTS . . . She pictured her parents in a car, lost but trying to find their way home. Then she stood up and made herself smile. "Who's Mrs. Birkenhead?"

"The housekeeper," said Sam. Then she added, "She's really more than a housekeeper. She's . . . well, she used to be my nanny, but I'm too old for that now."

"Is she nice?"

"Sure. Almost like a mother," Sam said briefly, turning to look for more sticks.

They gathered up the smaller sticks and stacked them near the woodpile next to the barn. "Nice barn," said Sam.

"That's where my mom and I fixed up the stall for my horse," said Anna, "before . . . before they left." Sam waited politely for her to continue, and before Anna knew it she was telling Sam about H-Rose and about the scrubbing and the sanding and the painting. She smiled sadly, remembering how hard she and her mother had laughed when a mouse ran across the floor, startling them so much that they both dropped their paintbrushes.

"Can I see?" asked Sam.

Anna hesitated. She hadn't been in the barn since that last time with her mother. "You mean the horse stall?" she said, frowning slightly.

"Never mind," Sam said quickly.

But Anna made a decision. "No, it's fine. I'd like to show you." Feeling strangely apprehensive, she walked over to the barn door and lifted the latch. Sam was right behind her. The door swung open.

Anna gasped. Towering over them, reaching all the way to the ceiling and tipping toward them as if it might tumble down, leaned a mountain of boxes and bags. A piano had been shoved into a corner. It was covered with chairs and more boxes. In another corner was the family computer, facedown on a footstool, which teetered on her mom's favorite rocking chair. She knew all of these things. They were from her old life.

"It's all here," she whispered. "Not at the

dump." She stood in silence as the familiar objects came into focus one by one. The photograph albums . . . Her father's fishing equipment . . . Her old schoolwork . . . It was all here, all here.

The movers appeared to have thrown everything in the barn in great haste. Aunt Formaldy no doubt had said to them, "These things will never do! They are not authentic. Please remove them, I do not care where. And do it quickly."

One of Anna's old Suzy dolls lay on her face next to the computer. She was covered in dust. Anna picked her up and brushed the dust off. She used to love her. She still did, she suddenly realized, and hugged her.

Sam was fingering a pile of old newspapers. She glanced up at Anna.

"I have a Suzy doll, too," she said suddenly. "Her name's Sarah. What's yours?"

"Emily," Anna said, picking spiderwebs out of the long dark hair. "I was wondering where she was." Emily's little shoes were missing, and her green jacket had slipped down over her shoulders. Anna buttoned the tiny top button of the jacket and tucked her shirt back in.

Sam bent down and picked up something from the floor. She gazed at it for a moment and then

brushed off the cobwebs with her sleeve before hand-
ing it to Anna. It was a silver-framed photograph.

"Are those your parents? They look nice."

Anna drew in her breath. Her mother and father,
their arms around Anna, smiled out at her, just as
they did in her dreams.

"You should keep it next to your bed."

Anna looked at the picture again. How could she
ever have thought she had forgotten? They were just
as they always had been—her father's big loving
smile, her mother's long red hair shining in the sunlight. Anna closed her eyes. She could almost hear
her mother's voice singing to her again: *"What'll I
do-oo-o with just a pho-to-graaaph . . ."*

"I miss them," she said in a low voice.

Sam nodded. "You can tell they love you." Her
voice sounded wistful.

Sam moved away and started brushing cobwebs
off the piano. There were cobwebs on everything.
And dust. Anna thought how strange it was, seeing
her past all jumbled up here as if it were just . . . junk.
But it wasn't junk, even if her aunt thought it was.

When she saw the fishing vest, she smiled, but
with a lump in her throat. Her father had looked
ridiculous in it, with its bulging pockets and high
waist and hooks sticking out everywhere. Anna and
her mother laughed at him every time he wore it.

Sometimes he would put it on even if he wasn't going fishing, just to make them laugh.

And there were her mother's old gardening gloves. Anna picked one up, remembering that her mother had never seen the daisies she had planted back in the spring.

"I wonder where Mom's little boxes are," said Anna, suddenly remembering them. "She collected them—different boxes from all over the world . . . Morocco, Japan, India, Egypt . . ." Anna had peeked into them when she was little. She never knew what she would find—buttons, safety pins, foreign coins, thumbtacks in the smaller ones; scarves, photographs, papers in the larger ones. There was a papier-mâché box from India that her mother had always put butterscotch candies in. And a tiny red velvet box that contained a glass heart.

"We haven't looked in that old trunk over there," suggested Sam, pointing to a dark shape in the corner.

It was an old-fashioned trunk, the kind sailors used to pack things in when they went to sea. Anna had never seen it before. Now a strange feeling came over her.

She hesitated for a moment. Then she strode over to the trunk and opened it.

THE
BOX

There were her mother's boxes—tin ones, wooden ones, plain and fancy.

And a large, unfamiliar-looking box.

It was made of shiny black ebony with red roses painted on the lid, the leaves inlaid with mother-of-pearl. The corners were chipped, the lid was dented, and it was covered with cobwebs. It smelled musty. But Anna could tell it had once been very beautiful. Through the dirt and dust, the red roses with their mother-of-pearl leaves glowed. A silver key was in the lock, and Anna turned it.

To most people the contents would have looked quite ordinary. There were papers and books and letters, some of them yellowed with age. But Anna felt her heart skip a beat. As she picked up a packet of papers, her hands were shaking. "This is Dad's hand-

writing," she said slowly. "He has the worst handwriting in the world. Mom always complains she
can't read it." The papers were covered with scrib-
blings. "Dad keeps lots of notes about everything.
He's a biologist."

She squinted, trying to make out the sharp, sloping handwriting. "Let's see . . . His writing is impossible!" She read as well as she could: "Hereditary
variability . . . speciation . . . isolation . . . reductive
properties. Oh, they're just biology notes," she said,
disappointed.

"Here's a map," said Sam, unfolding a large piece
of paper.

They looked at it curiously. It had been drawn in
pencil and seemed to represent a coastline with many
small islands scattered about.

"Maybe it's a treasure map," said Sam.

When Anna leaned over to peer at it, she noticed
an odd-looking volume in the corner of the box.
"What's this?"

She removed it carefully. The cover was brown
leather, worn and ancient-looking, the edges brittle
and jagged. Gold letters on the front said:

Diary 1771
Lucinda Anna Farrington

"My great-great-great-great grandmother's diary!" said Anna, astonished. "She was the first one to live in this house." She ran her fingers over the gold letters, then carefully opened the book.

"Child!" It was Aunt Formaldy calling from the house. "Child! Come and say hello to my good friends the Barnstables!"

Anna groaned. Her aunt just wanted to show her friends what a good aunt she was, she thought angrily. How was it that her aunt had any friends at all? Couldn't everyone see that she was a fake, a phony, a —?

"Child!" Aunt Formaldy's voice had a sharp edge to it, a dangerous sign.

"I've got to go," Anna said. She put the book back in the box and closed it with the key.

"See you tomorrow at school?" Sam said. Then she bent down and picked up a piece of paper from the floor and handed it to Anna.

"Sure, thanks." Anna stuffed the paper into her sweatshirt pocket. She smiled at her friend and then ran as fast as she could across the yard to the house, turning once to wave at Sam, who was climbing the fence to the old Claiborne backyard.

Aunt Formaldy was standing in the hallway, dressed in a cashmere coat and wearing a black beret. In her high-heeled boots, she towered over her friends.

"For goodness' sake, child! You are covered in dirt!" she cried, taking a step backward. Her forced smile was brighter than ever.

Anna glanced down at her shirt and pants. They were plastered with dust and cobwebs, and her hands were black with dirt. She tried to brush them off, but Aunt Formaldy's smile grew even brighter. "Not in the house, *dear* child!"

Aunt Formaldy turned to her guests, shook her head sorrowfully, and sighed. "Niece. Please say hello to the Barnstables." She half smiled at her company, as if they must understand what a trial it was to care for a girl like Anna.

Anna dutifully opened her mouth to say hello, but Aunt Formaldy swept on. "I am so sorry that I won't be able to have dinner with you, child," she said, as if the two of them routinely ate together. "I've left something delicious in the oven for you."

She took a last look in the mirror and smiled at her reflection. "You look flushed, my dear," she said, her voice ringing now like little bells. "Are you quite well?" She laid a cold, clammy hand across Anna's forehead.

"I'm fine," said Anna, trying not to recoil. How could a hand feel so much like a dead fish?

"Well, good then." Aunt Formaldy swept out the

door, the Barnstables hurrying in her wake. The required review was over.

"Fake!" Anna whispered.

And then she made a mistake. Instead of waiting to make sure Aunt Formaldy was safely gone, she ran back to the horse stall and picked up the mysterious box.

She was just hurrying up the stairs with it when Aunt Formaldy reappeared in the hallway.

"What have you got there?" Aunt Formaldy's voice sliced through the silence. The bells of just a minute ago were gone. Her appearance was so sudden that for a minute Anna wondered if she'd been lying in wait.

"I-I . . . " she stammered, trying to hide the mysterious box behind her.

Aunt Formaldy held out her hands. "I will dispose of that, if you don't mind," she said, wrinkling her nose.

Anna considered running down the stairs and out the door, or running up the stairs and hiding the box. Instead, she reluctantly handed it to her aunt and watched her move off in the direction of the great room.

Anna did not dare to follow her, except with her ears. She could hear her aunt's heels striking the floor impatiently and receding into the distance. What room was she in now? The family room? The great room? The dining room? There were so many rooms to choose from. There was silence for a moment, and then Anna could hear the footsteps returning. She fled up the stairs and hid, listening.

"I am sorry to keep you, my dears," she could hear Aunt Formaldy say. There was some mumbling. "Oh yes, I found my gloves." She laughed gaily. A door slammed, and they were gone.

Anna ran down the stairs and peered out the window. They were driving away.

Where was the box? What could her aunt have done with it?

It was downstairs, that much Anna knew. She ran through the rooms, searching quickly. Nothing. Then she went back and slowly examined everything. She looked behind the sofa. It wasn't there. She climbed on the sofa and looked on the top shelf of the bookcase. She even looked in the fireplace. After an hour of searching, she was no closer to discovering the mysterious rose-covered treasure. Where could her aunt have hidden it?

It was late, and she was suddenly starving. Remembering the dinner her aunt had mentioned, Anna went to the kitchen and opened the oven door.

It was cold and empty. She opened the refrigerator. No dinner. "I didn't really believe it," Anna said to herself as she made a peanut butter sandwich. There wasn't even any jelly. It was not a good evening.

After dinner Anna went back to her search. Again she looked in every corner of every room of the house, but the box seemed to have vanished. She was about to start over when she heard a car door slam. Her aunt had returned.

Anna's heart sank. The search would have to be postponed. Maybe Sam could help her look tomorrow. She thought about Sam's helping her with the backyard today. The girl seemed awfully nice, not a bit stuck-up.

As Anna lay in bed that night, she wondered what the diary might say, what those biology notes might mean. She tried to remember the map. Was it really a treasure map? She would find that box, no matter what, she decided. She had to!

She had no way of knowing that quite soon finding the box would become a matter of life and death.

STRANGE
BIRDS

A soft cooing sound woke Anna. She had been dreaming she was riding a horse as fast as the wind, flying over the treetops. She tried to go back to sleep but heard the cooing noise again. It was coming from outside.

The clock on her bedside table read 2:42 a.m. She shivered. It was still dark out, and the night air was cold and damp. That noise—what was it? She listened carefully. It was a peculiar sound, foreign and familiar at the same time. Now there was rustling. Rustling and cooing. And it was right outside her window.

Her tree! Was something in her tree? She took her flashlight and crept over to the window, her heart beating fast. She listened. Yes—no doubt about it, something was there.

She strained her ears. No other sounds came from outside. Even the crickets were quiet. There was just that odd cooing and rustling in the leaves. She stepped into the tree and looked up. Was something moving up there? It was so dark she couldn't be sure. She turned on the flashlight and shone it into the upper branches.

A high-pitched cry cut through the night air, followed by a flurry of flapping and fluttering.

Anna was so shocked that she dropped her flashlight. With a pounding heart she picked it up and shone it into the tree again. Too late. Whatever it was, it was gone.

"Strange birds," said Anna out loud, her voice trembling. "Not birds from around here."

She went back to bed and lay in the dark, her eyes wide open. For a long time she waited for the cooing sounds to return. But it was quiet. And when the crickets started singing again, she fell asleep. She did not hear the strange birds return.

But they did.

"UNSAVORY" MEANS UNAPPETIZING

She took the box," Anna told her new friend the next day. They were having lunch together in the cafeteria. School had reopened, and everything was almost back to normal. The power was on, streets and yards had been cleaned up, and the large pools of water everywhere had shrunk to puddles.

"How did she find it?" asked Sam, taking a bite of her pizza.

"I was carrying it upstairs to my room," Anna replied sheepishly. She had been feeling bad all morning because she hadn't made sure Aunt Formaldy was gone before taking the box into the house.

"Well, it's somewhere," Sam said after a minute. "We'll find it."

Anna heard the "we" and said gratefully, "I sure hope so. But I've looked. I've looked and looked. It's nowhere." She felt her voice tremble, and she stopped.

"Hey," said Sam. "It's okay. I said we'll find it. So we will." She looked so sure about it that Anna smiled. "Say," Sam said, changing the subject, "did you hear those strange birds?"

"Birds?" Anna looked at her friend with surprise, suddenly remembering. She had almost decided she had dreamed those birds. "I heard something. They were in my . . . tree."

"I heard them this morning," said Sam.

"What kind are they?" asked Anna.

"I couldn't see them. Mrs. Birkenhead says they were probably blown here by the hurricane. You have very odd weather around here."

Anna suddenly remembered a news item her father had read to her once. One morning after a powerful storm had blown through, a woman in Maine had gone out her back door and found three pink flamingos drinking from her birdbath.

"They must be very unhappy," said Anna thoughtfully. "I mean, the lost birds. Greeley, New Hampshire, wouldn't be exactly what they're used to."

"I can imagine," Sam said.

Anna thought of the birds huddled together, frightened and hungry. "I wonder what they eat?" she said as the bell rang, announcing that lunch was over. She took a last gulp of her milk and wiped her mouth with her paper napkin. "Maybe I should start saving leftover pizza for them," she added as they slid their half-eaten pizza into the trash can. *Or for me*, she thought, remembering how tired she was of peanut butter sandwiches.

When they returned to the classroom, Walker was standing in the middle of a group of students. "My uncle's circus is so cool," he was saying. "He owns the whole thing. Plus he's the Ringmaster."

"I love circuses," Stacy gushed.

"Well, they're setting up tonight and opening first thing tomorrow morning."

"My mom says she voted against allowing the circus in town," said Avery. Avery's mother was one of the selectmen. "She says it's unsavory."

"Unsavory. Huh. Rhymes with Avery," said Walker, grinning.

"They're only allowed to stay one day," Avery went on. "The selectmen were very strict about it."

"Is it a three-ring circus?" asked Eric.

"Three rings are stupid," Walker said. "A three-ring circus is for suckers." He gave Eric a shrewd look. "You like three-ring circuses?"

Eric shrugged.

Walker continued. "My uncle has the weirdest animals. You should see them. Ever hear of a wombat?"

No one had.

"Hey," he said, "I'll bet I can get tickets for the whole class." He looked over at Anna and Sam, who were standing together on the other side of the room. "Well, not the *whole* class," he said with a sneer.

The circus came in the night, five trucks and a few vans rattling through the center of the village onto Mrs. Perry's field. Except for the brightly colored sign on one of the trucks—CECIL STROMWOLD'S STUPENDOUS CIRCUS!—it did not look very promising. The first truck was missing a fender and had a large dent in the hood. A pipe hung down from beneath the second truck, scraping the ground and spewing a cloud of black smoke. The third truck had plastic taped over two of its windows.

As soon as they reached the field, a work crew set up their advertising: a large pair of searchlights. The bright beams sliced through the night sky, two swords of light crossing and recrossing over Greeley, announcing the arrival of Cecil Stromwold and his Stupendous Circus.

Anna could see the lights from the lookout high in her tree. But instead of looking pretty and festive, she thought they looked cold and mean.

CECIL STROMWOLD'S STUPENDOUS CIRCUS

Anna took a bite of cereal and chewed it slowly, feeling restless and worried. For once she couldn't concentrate on the book she was reading. Where was the box? When would she get another chance to look for it? Yesterday after school Aunt Formaldy had been entertaining the Historical Society. Today she had spread out wallpaper books and seemed to be ready to spend the day studying them. More waiting. Anna sighed.

It was Saturday, and that meant the circus was in town. Even though she was sure it would be a very poor one, it was, after all, a circus. Would everyone from her class be there?

The doorbell rang and Anna paused, spoon halfway to mouth. She wasn't supposed to answer the door. Her aunt had made that very clear. "You will have no reason to," she had pointed out.

The doorbell rang again.

Now Anna heard her aunt's sharp footsteps hit the well-polished wooden floors as she approached the front door. Anna shrugged and continued eating.

"Hi, I'm Sam—is Anna here?"

"No, there's nobody here by that name, young man," she heard her aunt say.

"I brought today's paper," Sam said. "It's got your tree on the front page."

"Oh, so it does—just the tree, though." She sounded annoyed. "Thank you very much, quite kind of you."

The door closed with a bang and Anna heard Aunt Formaldy's footsteps on the stairs. She jumped up from her chair and hurried to the front door. She cracked it open and peered out. Sam was still standing on the stoop, looking baffled.

"Hi, Sam," said Anna, so happy to see her friend that she grinned from ear to ear.

"Was that your aunt?" Sam asked.

"Aunt Formaldy," said Anna, making a face.

Sam glanced at the house. "She doesn't seem to know you're here."

"I don't think she knows I exist," Anna agreed. "Maybe I'm invisible."

"You're not invisible to me," Sam said. "Just to

her. But that might come in handy sometime—like when we look for the box."

Anna shook her head and stepped out the front door. "We can't look now. She's in decorating mode. I think she'll be here all day."

"Are you allowed to go to the circus?" Sam asked suddenly.

It had been a long time since Anna had asked permission to go anywhere. Why, she imagined that if she disappeared into thin air, it might be weeks before her aunt noticed.

"Sure," she said casually, but she was excited. "Maybe when we get back she'll be gone."

A gust of chilly air scattered a pile of leaves and Anna shivered. "I'd better get a jacket." She looked at Sam's bare arms. Sam was wearing an embroidered yellow vest over a purple T-shirt. "You want to borrow something?"

Sam looked down at herself and nodded. "Sure. Thanks."

Anna dashed around to the back of the house, ran upstairs, and came back with two sweatshirts.

"Why did you go all the way around the house?" asked Sam, gratefully slipping the red one over her vest. "Or, wait, let me guess—you're not allowed in the front door?"

Anna made a wry face. "At least I'm allowed in the back door."

Sam shook her head wonderingly. "And people think your aunt is so nice."

"She's good at pretending," Anna said, happy that at last someone besides herself knew what a fraud her aunt was.

"One of these days people will find out," Sam said grimly.

Anna shook her head. "I wonder."

Mrs. Perry's field was less than a mile away, through the village. Groups of people were headed in the same direction, including Walker, Stacy, and Avery. Walker sneered at the girls before turning back to his friends.

The leaves on the trees had already started to turn yellow and red. The hurricane had blown many to the ground, and the village green was covered with them.

"New Hampshire," Sam said. "It looks like a postcard."

They heard the circus before they saw it. A calliope wailed out of tune, and a man could be heard shouting something over a loudspeaker about "amazing feats and horrifying freaks." Although

Walker's descriptions of the circus had sounded pathetic, Anna was looking forward to it now. It was a beautiful fall day, she had a friend, and the smell of popcorn and fried dough began to drift toward them.

But when Anna saw the shabby wagons and frayed tents, her heart sank. A zoolike smell hung over the trucks, and she thought of the animals Walker had said would be there. "The best part of the circus," he had said. She doubted it.

Families with small children hurried to get good seats in the center tent. Anna and Sam followed along behind. They arrived just in time for the big-top performance. It was so dimly lighted they could barely make out the large ring in the center, with ropes dangling high above. A shaft of daylight shone through a rip at the top of the tent. The air smelled of mildew.

Suddenly a drum roll announced the beginning of the show and a bright spotlight revealed the Ringmaster, dressed in a glittering suit and a top hat.

"Ladies and gentlemen!" he shouted. "Welcome to Cecil Stromwold's Stupendous Circus!"

Anna peered at him. The Ringmaster was extremely tall and thin, with dark hair. His face, however, was round and pudgy and looked out of place on his body. He had small, glittering eyes, which caught the light. Anna thought they looked mean. She could see the family resemblance to Walker even from where they were sitting.

"That must be Walker's uncle," she whispered.

The Ringmaster held out his arms to welcome the crowd and threw his head back. "Ladies and gentlemen!" he repeated. "Let the circus begin!"

Then he cracked his whip and a bright spotlight burst onto six three-legged dogs wearing clown hats. They hobbled into the ring in close formation, nose to tail. Their heads were down and their tails drooped between their legs. A drum roll rumbled again, introducing a pale elephant with a giant flowered hat perched on her head. The elephant's large feet were cracked and covered with sores, and she stumbled on the beaten-down grass. She looked old and plodded along as if every step was an effort. Finally, a bear dressed in a clown suit and wearing a chain around his neck lumbered into the ring, swinging his head slowly from side to side. His fur was dirty and matted. Little flies buzzed around his eyes.

The animals trotted around the circle to a scratchy recording of "Teddy Bear's Picnic." The Ringmaster, his eyes glinting in the spotlight, cracked his whip again, and all the animals reversed direction.

Anna and Sam looked at each other. Without a word, they stood up and walked out.

"Those poor animals! What a way to treat them," said Sam.

Anna shook her head. "He's mean. Just like Walker."

As they walked away from the tent, Anna could hear scattered applause. "Ladies and gentlemen, I now direct your attention to . . ." The Ringmaster's voice faded into the fall day, which no longer seemed quite so beautiful to Anna.

ANNA'S ROOM

It was not until they had left the popcorn smell and the calliope music far behind that either of them spoke again. "Can you keep a secret?" Anna asked Sam.

"Of course."

"I want to show you something," Anna announced.

They went through the back door of the Farrington house. Anna whispered, "We have to take our shoes off." Carrying their shoes, they tiptoed past the elegant drawing room and the heavily draped dining room. The *Greeley Times* lay on the table. It was wrinkled, as if someone had crumpled it in anger, but the girls could still read it. There was a picture of Anna's tree on the front page:

THE CASE TREE STANDS!

Greeley braced for Bela on Wednesday, and when all was said and done, 547 trees were downed, power was lost to 8,000 homes, and the Souhegan River overflowed its banks. But Greeley's famous Justin Case Tree weathered the storm.

Aunt Formaldy's voice came suddenly from the living room. "Well, yes, the front page, but I am a little surprised that they did not print the picture they took of me standing in front of it." She sounded annoyed.

"Come on!" Anna whispered as she led the way upstairs to her bedroom. She opened the door and squeezed in around the bed.

"This is your room?" asked Sam, looking at the cramped space.

"It's *part* of my room," said Anna. "The best part is over here." Then she threw the window up and stepped out into the tree.

Sam's eyes opened wide as she slowly took in the tables and shelves, the books and games, the box of cookies, the sofa and chairs, the tea set, the cushions and hammock, the stairs and the railings in the tree. She reached out her hand and ran it along a branch overhead. She felt one of the leaves, rubbing it between her fingers. She shook her head and, letting out a low whistle, turned around to look at Anna. "Amazing," she said. "It's . . . *amazing*."

"Want to see upstairs?" asked Anna. They climbed the stairs to the top of the tree, past the reading corner and the hidden hammock, to the lookout. Anna pushed apart the leaves and they peered out of the small opening at the top. In the distance, Mount Monadnock stood tall and bald. Red and yellow trees covered its sides. The autumn sun was low in the sky, and its rays were golden for miles around.

Sam turned and gazed at the wooden platform she was standing on and then back at the mountain.

"I have the feeling your aunt doesn't know about this," she said.

Anna shook her head. "You and I are the only ones, except my friend Beth, who moved just before you arrived, and my parents. If Aunt Formaldy ever found out . . ."

Sam frowned. "Don't worry. We won't let her."

"You know something?" Anna said suddenly. "I thought you were stuck-up before."

Her friend stared at her. "Me? I thought *you* were stuck-up!" They looked at each other and then both burst out laughing. "Well," Sam said at last, "it just goes to show you."

"It just shows to go-ya!" Anna agreed, and they started laughing again.

"So, what's up with your aunt?" Sam asked, becoming serious. "Is she always hanging around the house like today?"

"Hardly ever, actually. Unless she's entertaining the Historical Society. I think she's trying to be their next president." Anna sighed, and then she brightened. "She's always gone on Sundays. That's tomorrow. Do you want to look for the box then?"

Sam shook her head. "My parents are coming home tomorrow." She said "home" as if it were in quotation marks. "I'll help you on Monday after school, though. They'll be back in Washington by then." A wistful look crossed her face. "They never stay around long."

"Maybe I'll find it before then," Anna said. "I have a feeling Sunday's going to be a special day."

Anna turned out to be right about Sunday. But not in the way she expected.

THE NOISE
AGAIN

That night Anna lay in bed thinking about how good it felt to have a friend again. She thought about the look Sam had had when she stepped into the tree. Sharing the tree with someone made her happy. She closed her eyes, reliving each moment.

For a second the image of the tired animals at the circus broke through her thoughts. She saw the Ringmaster's cruel mouth and shuddered.

She wouldn't think about that. Instead she would think about the delicious feeling of having a friend, of talking again, of even laughing . . .

She sat up in bed. There was that noise. The cooing sound—oddly familiar and yet foreign. The strange birds. They had come back.

They were in her tree, she was certain, and they were scared. They must be. Lost and far from home—of course they were scared.

They probably aren't flamingos, she decided. She would have liked it if they were. But possibly they were exotic parrots from Central America. Or wild parakeets.

Whatever they were, they must be hungry. She could find out what parrots or parakeets eat and take them food. It would be fun to have a tree full of parrots. She could teach them words and talk to them.

She slipped out of bed, pushed aside the curtain, and stepped into the tree, being careful to be as silent as possible. She looked up at the branches overhead. It was dark, but not too dark to see.

There was a flock of them, and they hovered over her head. They were not parrots. They were not wild parakeets.

They were—Anna blinked her eyes—horses!

Beautiful, perfect horses. Except each one was only ten inches high. And each one had wings.

They hovered and flitted, suspended overhead like ornaments in a tree. Their wings were silky, not transparent but almost, so delicate they seemed colorless, yet sparkling, like dew on spiderwebs.

Anna rubbed her eyes. They were as real as she was, living, breathing creatures flitting delicately from branch to branch, their tiny hooves resting softly on the tree, their wings moving gently, like butterfly wings. There were mares and fillies and colts. Each one was different. And each more beautiful than the last. They had coats of gold and silver, white and black and chestnut. One colt had spots, like an Appaloosa. Their flowing manes and tails looked as soft as silk. Their eyes were large and brown, and they regarded Anna warily.

High overhead a mare as black as ink stood with her head down. She hadn't seemed to notice Anna.

Very slowly, trying not to make any sudden movement, Anna sat down. She watched them, her brain a muddle of thoughts and questions. Where were they from? Why were they so small? How did they get wings? What were they doing here? Now she realized that the cooing sound was very much like neighing, only smaller and higher pitched.

The horses seemed to be grazing. *They like the nutberries*, thought Anna. She watched as they flicked their tails gently and stretched their graceful necks to pluck off the small nuts. They looked for all the world like horses out to pasture on a soft summer day.

Except for the wings. Except for the fact that this was not a pasture. It was a tree.

A high whinny sounded suddenly behind Anna. She turned and gasped when she saw the creature that stood there.

A stallion, tiny but much bigger than the other horses, and so white he was almost blue, reared up on his hind legs, his wings spread out behind him. He gazed fiercely at Anna, his eyes wide and flashing, his nostrils flared. She stared back at him, wondering if he was dangerous.

For a minute the two of them were as still as statues. At last the stallion nickered softly and nudged Anna with his little nose. Timidly she reached out her hand to touch him, and to her surprise he dropped something into it. He was offering her a nutberry.

Everything about him is real, thought Anna. Little ears, flicking forward and backward. Small body breathing in and out. Flowing mane and long tail, all miniaturized. His tiny hoof pawed the branch impatiently, as if he were waiting for her to do something. What?

He reminded her of a creature in a picture she had seen somewhere. Pegasus—the flying horse of Greek mythology. Anna remembered that her mother had had a book about Pegasus. It had been on her desk when she left on the fateful journey with Anna's father.

The stallion's dark eyes watched her intently, and Anna had the strange sensation that she could almost read his thoughts.

He's trying to tell me something.

He pawed the tree branch again, then flew up to the higher branch where the black mare stood. He looked down at Anna, then he reared on his hind legs and pawed the branch again, his wings moving slowly back and forth.

He wants to show me something.

Anna hurried up the stairs to where the two horses were. What she saw made her gasp again.

BLOOD

It was a tiny colt, as white as the stallion except for a black blaze running down his nose like a streak of lightning. He was lying on a pile of dried grass and straw. His chest heaved and his eyes were closed. As she watched, a shiver racked his body and he opened his eyes briefly. They were wide and terrified. But it was the blood that shocked Anna, the blood that oozed out of the little colt's side and the pool of it that had thickened and darkened on the branch.

"What happened to you?" She bent down slowly over the tiny body, the black mare snorting nervously at her side, the stallion fluttering overhead. Blood had always made Anna sick—the sight of her own, the sight of others'. She felt her head swim for a minute as she peered at a long gash in the colt's left side.

Then she took a deep breath and tried to clear her head. How deep was the gash? Was he dying? Could she help? She started to reach over to part the glossy white hair and saw the dirt under her fingernails. *I have to wash my hands or he'll get infected,* she thought.

She must hurry, hurry. She fled down the stairs to the window level, entered her room, and tiptoed out into the hallway, listening closely. Aunt Formaldy's snores rumbled out of her bedroom and down the hall. Swiftly, Anna went into the bathroom and gathered supplies: water, soap, a washcloth, antiseptic, gauze, tape. Wait, she had to wash her hands. Setting everything down on the edge of the sink, she quickly scrubbed her hands. *Hurry! Hurry!* she thought, and in her rush, the supplies she'd collected fell with a crash! The sudden noise made her jump, and she bent down and gathered everything up as quickly as she could.

She sneaked back into the hall, but something was wrong. The loud snoring had stopped. Before Anna had a chance to do anything, a light went on in the hallway.

"What on earth?" Aunt Formaldy stood in the doorway.

"I was just getting a drink of water," said Anna as calmly as she could manage.

"In the future you will wait until morning, young lady. Such rudeness, getting up in the middle of the night like that! Goodness knows when I'll be able to get back to sleep now." Aunt Formaldy crossed her arms over her chest. "Go to bed. Now."

What would her aunt do if she found out about the creatures? Anna winced at the thought. She would have to wait until her aunt fell back asleep before she returned to the tree. In an agony of impatience she went to her room, leaving her door ajar so she could see when her aunt's light went off. Aunt Formaldy had not noticed the first aid equipment. No doubt some unconscious calculation in her brain computed, "Injury + Anna = Unimportant."

But was she listening now?

It was ten minutes, ten excruciatingly long minutes, before Aunt Formaldy's snores filled the house once more. With fumbling fingers, Anna gathered up her first aid supplies and stepped out her window into the tree. All was quiet. She shone her flashlight up into the branches.

There was nothing. They were gone.

A fierce anger filled Anna. Never had she felt so much like throwing things at her aunt as she did now.

The beautiful creatures were gone, and it was Aunt Formaldy's fault.

Then a small sound, a whimper, came from above. Anna ran up the stairs, and there was the colt, all alone, breathing heavily. Had his parents abandoned him? She bent down and touched him gently to calm him. Blood still oozed out of his gash, and Anna's head swam. She patted the area with the wet cloth. The cut was deep. How deep? she wondered. Did it go all the way to his insides?

With soap and water she washed the wound clean. Blood continued to drip out of it, but not as much as before. *I can't believe I am doing this*, thought Anna, feeling as though she were outside herself, watching from a nearby branch. She no longer felt like fainting. On the contrary, she felt calm.

Anna applied the antiseptic and then ever so gently put a strip of gauze on top. Instantly it turned bright red, shockingly bright against the white. She unrolled more and more gauze until it stayed white, and then with one hand she carefully lifted the tiny colt so she could wind the bandage around him. The small body felt so alive, so *breathing*, that Anna gasped. "Please don't die," she whispered.

Where were the others? Why had they left him?

Suddenly she remembered that Sam had heard the strange birds in her backyard. Had they returned there? Why? She tried to picture Sam's yard, the old oak tree, the tire swing, the birdbath . . .

The birdbath! And instantly it was clear to her.

They have to search for water. That was it. Anna was certain of it. They must have been incredibly thirsty to have left the injured colt behind.

As soon as she thought of water, Anna felt a rush of panic—what about the colt? He must be thirsty, too. Maybe he was dying, literally dying, of thirst.

Again Anna hurried back into the house. This time, as quiet as dust, she tiptoed downstairs and filled a shallow bowl with water. Back upstairs, she took an eyedropper out of the medicine cabinet in the bathroom and hurried to the tree.

The colt was still breathing, but the white gauze was red again, dark red. Filling the dropper with water, Anna gently lifted the colt's head. Although his eyes were closed, he drank eagerly. She filled the dropper again, and again he drank. At last his thirst seemed to be quenched, and Anna sighed.

Sitting by his side and stroking his head, she whispered, "Hush little one, everything will be all right." *Please let that be true*, she thought as she watched the tiny horse struggle for breath.

"H-Rose," she said suddenly, naming the tiny creature. She ran her finger gently along his side. His little body felt like a small furnace. "H-Rose," she whispered again.

An owl hooted in the distance, and Anna jumped. Suddenly she knew what had happened to the little colt. He had been attacked. Maybe by an owl, maybe by something else.

It isn't safe out there, she thought. It isn't safe at all.

Where were the others? she wondered anxiously. How long did it take to fly to Sam's birdbath and back?

The minutes dragged by. Once she heard an animal cry out—in pain? The church clock struck two. A car swished down the street in front of her house. What was taking them so long? *What if they never came back?*

Just as Anna began to fear the worst, she heard a muffled crash overhead. The small horses were back, hurtling through the leaves like a hail of arrows, showering small twigs and nutberries onto her head. She shut her eyes.

When she opened them, the white stallion and the black mare were already hovering over the little sleeping colt, inspecting the new white bandage suspiciously. The stallion turned his gaze to Anna.

"It's okay," she whispered.

The rest of the horses settled down onto the welcoming branches of the tree like birds coming home to roost. They seem to feel at home here, she thought. *It was as if they belonged here.*

One by one the horses dozed off, and at last so did Anna, her cheek pressed into a nubby branch, the leaves rustling their old lullaby.

CYCLONE

Ping! Something fell on Anna's head. Ping! Something else, this time on her arm. She opened an eye. It was morning, and the sun filtered in through the leaves, giving everything a warm green glow. Ping! What *was* that? Anna looked up. A leggy colt, as black as night with a white blaze, just the opposite of H-Rose, fluttered above her. He plucked a nutberry from an overhead branch and dropped it onto Anna's nose as she gazed up at him in amazement.

So she hadn't just dreamed the horses. They were real. She sat up, and the colt darted off to a higher branch and hid in a cluster of leaves. Her cheek was sore from the branch she had been sleeping on and she rubbed it, her gaze falling on H-Rose. He was asleep, breathing shallowly. With a start of guilt she realized she had slept for hours without thinking about him. Now she reached over and felt his body.

It was still hot. Very hot. She remembered her mother saying that you had to drink plenty of fluids when you had a fever. Gently lifting his tiny head with her finger, she gave the little colt five drops of water, then five more. He drank, but his eyes remained closed. Was there something else she should do?

"Sleep is good," she said to herself doubtfully. Wasn't it?

Anna looked around for the rest of the horses. And there, directly behind her, balancing on a branch, was the white stallion, watching her. How long had he been there?

"Oh!" exclaimed Anna, blushing for no reason. "I didn't know you were here." His dark brown eyes had flecks of gold in them. She held out her hand and he came closer, so close she could feel his warm breath.

"You should have a name," she murmured. He whinnied softly at the sound of her voice and fluttered his wings a few times. "Well," she went on, "since you came in a hurricane, I'll call you Cyclone. Do you like that?"

Cyclone nickered in reply and then flitted up to where H-Rose lay and looked down at Anna expectantly.

Anna changed H-Rose's bandages three more

times that day. She tried giving him nutberries, but he refused, accepting only water. Once he opened his eyes and once he raised his head halfheartedly, but mostly he slept. Whenever Anna came near him, his mother fluttered nervously about. Anna finished up as quickly as she could and climbed down to the sofa to sit and watch.

She held herself very still, wishing the horses would come closer. They peered down at her curiously from the upper branches. They seemed shy.

At last a reddish colt with a black tail and a black mane landed abruptly on Anna's lap. She caught her breath, hardly daring to breathe, and studied the small horse. He had such tiny hooves that she could barely feel them through her jeans. She noticed that he had four black socks. In a flash he settled down, tucking his legs under him as if he were quite comfortable and at home. He made a little noise, like a miniature whinny, and instantly an identical little colt flapped down from a branch overhead, tumbling onto Anna's lap like a wee little puppy dog. He turned his brown eyes up to her as if saying, "I can be here, too, can't I?"

Anna sat completely still, not moving a finger, wondering if her pounding heart would disturb the tiny creatures. But they seemed quite at home on her lap. They adjusted their weight a little to get more comfortable and made small satisfied noises as they gazed up at her, and after a few moments Anna began to relax, a strange sensation expanding inside her chest. It was a feeling she had not had in a long, long time. It was like drinking cocoa and eating cookies, it was like being sung to, it was—yes, it was a lot like happiness.

"You should have names, you know," said Anna contentedly. She stroked their heads with her finger, thinking. "How about Red Sox?" she said to the first colt, "since you're reddish and you have four socks." Red Sox stirred sleepily, sticking one tiny hoof out from under him, as if to say, "You're right! I do have socks!" She turned to his twin. "So that means I should call you Yankee."

Bit by bit the other horses fluttered down closer to Anna, eyeing her warily. Each one seemed to have its own personality. She would find names for all of them, she thought, once she got to know them better.

Anna shifted in her seat, reluctant to disturb the twin colts but worrying about H-Rose. "I'll be back," she whispered at last to the sleeping twins as she gently moved them. In an instant they were awake, their brown eyes startled. They fluttered up to the higher branches and looked down at Anna reproachfully.

H-Rose was so still when Anna reached him that

for a moment she feared he had stopped breathing. She looked at him intently, her heart pounding. His diminutive rib cage moved up and down in a sudden jerk, and she breathed a sigh of relief. He was still alive. She changed his bandages and gave him some water. He did not open his eyes once.

The black mare fluttered about anxiously, as if trying to decide whether to trust this giant person. "I'll take very good care of your little colt, I promise," Anna said in a soothing voice. She held out her hand to the worried mare, who nuzzled it with her tiny warm nose and then looked up at Anna with deep brown eyes.

"You're so beautiful—like Black Beauty," whispered Anna. "How about if I call you Beauty?" The mother horse whinnied and bent over her colt again. "Everything is going to be all right," Anna heard herself say. Again she hoped that was true.

Anna went back down the stairs to the sofa, and immediately the horses seemed to relax. They settled on the lower branches to watch. Red Sox and Yankee swooped down and landed clumsily on her lap again.

"Hi," Anna said softly. The twins snorted, stamped their tiny feet, and instantly fell asleep. *They trust me,* thought Anna in awe.

She gazed at the horses flitting in the branches

overhead. A golden mare and a silver filly stood side by side, so bright they almost glowed in the green leaves of the tree. "You must be Sunbeam and Moonbeam," said Anna in a soft voice. A timid colt with spots peeked out from behind a cluster of nut-berries and then quickly hid again. Anna smiled and whispered, "I'll call you Fugitive." The colt reappeared for a moment, blinked his big brown eyes at her, and disappeared again. Anna sighed contentedly. She wished this could last forever.

Cyclone, who had accompanied her when she went to check on H-Rose, settled onto the arm of the sofa.

"Just where did all of you come from?" Anna asked.

The stallion tossed his head and whinnied, snorting air out his nostrils.

Anna studied him. The hurricane must have blown the winged horses here from a place so far away that nobody had ever heard of them. If anyone had, Anna would have, too. Creatures this rare would be known around the world. She would have seen pictures of them, maybe even movies.

People would try to capture them and keep them.

This thought filled her with such a sudden panic that she jumped up, scaring the horses into the upper branches, where they hovered nervously, peering down at her. Except for Cyclone, who watched her, and Beauty, who stood faithfully by her colt.

"I'm sorry!" said Anna in a gentle voice. She sat back down. "You can come back now!" And they did, flitting softly onto her lap.

They were so delicate and fragile that it almost hurt to look at them. What would happen to these beautiful creatures when people found out about them? Anna knew the answer: they would be captured and put on display, or even worse. Thinking of something like that happening to the winged horses made her feel sick.

Then another awful thought struck her. What if someone else had *already* seen them? What if someone was planning on capturing them at this very moment? The creatures had been here since the hurricane—that was five days ago. Anyone might have seen the horses as they searched for water.

Anna held her breath and listened. Was someone out on the sidewalk right now, scrutinizing her tree? Was that the sound of low breathing? Footsteps?

No, it was just her imagination. She looked at Cyclone and hoped that she was the only person in the world who knew.

It was getting dark, and Anna watched the horses

anxiously. They had not left the tree all day. Would they leave now that it was almost night? But they drank the water she had put out for them and at last they settled down. Except for Cyclone, who seemed to be standing guard.

He thinks they are in danger, Anna thought. *And they are.*

BAD NEWS

Two items of bad news greeted Anna the next morning at school. Sam was home sick. And that horrible circus was still in town.

"Boy, is my mom ever mad!" said Avery excitedly. "She says the circus was supposed to leave on Sunday and today is Monday and it's still here. She and the rest of the selectmen are going to ask the police to *make* it leave. She said that the circus owner is acting really strange and making stupid excuses about why they're all still here."

"My uncle never does anything stupid," objected Walker. "Besides, what's the big deal? They've taken down the circus, haven't they? They just haven't left yet." Walker looked around as if daring anyone to criticize his uncle. "I wish he'd set everything up again so we could go see the show tonight," he said.

"Ooh, that would be so good!" said Stacy. "I loved those cute little doggies."

Avery looked at her best friend in disgust. "The police would never let them set up again. It's against the agreement they made with the town. In fact," she said triumphantly, "I bet they've already called the police."

Everyone in Anna's class seemed happy at the thought of something happening that involved the police. The town of Greeley did not see much police action. The last time Anna had even seen a policeman was when one came to her elementary school to talk about bicycle safety.

"Maybe they'll handcuff your uncle and take him to jail," Zachary said to Walker.

"Does your uncle have a gun?" wondered Noah.

"Maybe—and if they try to push my uncle around, they'll be sorry. He's really something when he's mad," Walker boasted. "And he always gets his way," he added darkly.

As Anna listened to the conversation from the other side of the room, a sick feeling grew in her stomach. Something bad was going to happen, she just knew it.

Ms. Pritz brought the class to order. "I am sure you all remember that tomorrow is teachers' conference day," she said. "And that means no school!"

Everyone cheered.

"I guess I'll just have to hang out at my uncle's circus," Walker said.

"Can I come?" begged Stacy.

Walker shook his head. "Nope. He's up to something, and I'm going to find out what."

Anna started. Up to something? Could he have seen the horses? Then she reassured herself that she was the only one who knew about them. Still, she wished she were with them, protecting them, instead of sitting here in this dumb class. Would H-Rose even be alive when she got back? Would all the others still be in her tree?

QUICK THINKING

As soon as school was over, Anna hurried home.

"The Morrisons are picking me up at three-thirty." Aunt Formaldy's voice came from the living room. She was talking on the phone again. "Although I see that it is already four minutes past three-thirty."

Anna tiptoed to the stairs.

"Now that's an odd sight—a strange man is walking down my street with a butterfly net."

Anna froze. *A butterfly net?*

"Yes, he's out there now . . ."

Anna crept to the doorway and peered into the living room. Her aunt was wearing her long black coat and black gloves. She held the phone in one hand and was holding back the lace curtain with the other, staring out the window. Anna's mother's pearl necklace glowed in a beam of sunlight.

"I do not think strangers should roam freely about our town, do you? He certainly is tall and thin," she added, as if that were solid proof of his criminal nature.

Anna's blood froze. The Ringmaster! He was looking for the horses, she was sure of it! A vision of caged horses, miniature whips, and gaping spectators filled Anna with horror.

Her aunt spoke again. "The police? Oh my, no. No need to call them at all!" She laughed her tinkly laugh. "I will simply speak to him myself."

Anna ducked into the dining room just as her aunt swept out of the house, slamming the door behind her. What if the horses flew out of the tree right now? She ran to the living room and pulled back the curtain to look out the window. Aunt Formaldy, her long black coat billowing behind her, strode down the sidewalk.

"Excuse me, sir!" Anna heard her call out. The man turned around. It *was* Walker's uncle! She watched as he bowed to her aunt and smiled. They exchanged a few words. Finally the Ringmaster bowed again and turned to cross the street. Aunt Formaldy glared at his retreating back, then walked briskly to the house. Anna fled up the stairs just as her aunt opened the front door.

The phone rang. "Hello—oh, that is quite all right, my dear Mrs. Morrison. Five minutes is fine. I am actually thankful that you are late. I had a chance to meet a very interesting birdwatcher . . . Yes, I'll tell you all about it when you get here. Apparently we have some strange birds in our neighborhood!" Aunt Formaldy's laugh bounced off the walls and up the stairs.

So he does know about the horses, Anna thought in dismay. *And he's trying to catch them for his circus!*

Anna, who had sneaked halfway down the stairs to eavesdrop on her aunt, now ran up them two at a time, slipped into her room, and hurried out the window and into her tree. She looked around. The horses were all there, flitting restlessly from branch to branch.

"Shhhhh," whispered Anna. "Don't make a sound." She tiptoed up the stairs to where the black mare stood guard and peered down at H-Rose. The colt seemed even smaller and frailer than before. With fumbling hands, she gave him water from the eyedropper. Cyclone, watching her from the branch above, beat his wings back and forth furiously.

"He's out there, isn't he?" whispered Anna. She

hurried up the stairs to the lookout, her heart pounding. The lookout was high enough so she could see a long distance, but to see below her she had to walk to the end of the platform and lean over slightly. A car was just pulling up to the front of the house, and she watched as her aunt slipped inside, laughing gaily. The car pulled away from the curb and disappeared around the corner. Anna sighed with relief. There was no sign of the Ringmaster.

But then a movement down the street caught her eye. He hadn't left after all. He was studying every tree on the street, looking up into their branches, shading his eyes from the sun.

Anna watched helplessly as he approached her house, gazing up at the tree. He was whistling. Although she knew he couldn't see her, she ducked down, her mind racing.

What if the horses flew out of the tree right now? Was there anything she could do? How did he know about the horses? she wondered. She was certain that they were what he was looking for.

Maybe she could lead him someplace else, trick him into thinking the horses were there instead of here. But where?

Anna hurried down from the lookout to the branch where the horses were. Cyclone seemed more anxious than ever. What if he flew away? What if the Ringmaster saw him? Anna's legs felt like rubber. But she had made a decision.

She scrambled out of the tree, down the stairs, and out the front door before she could change her mind.

The tall figure stepped back from the sidewalk and pressed himself against a tree. Anna pretended she didn't see him. She looked around furtively, as if she had a secret. Then, turning away from the Ringmaster, she hurried down the street, glancing from side to side like a person afraid of being observed. She stopped to tie her shoe and managed to catch a glimpse of the Ringmaster slinking along behind her. Her trick was working. He was following her.

Anna's mind was racing. She would lead the Ringmaster to the old Grummer place on the other side of the village. She used to play there sometimes as a little girl. It was the perfect spot, full of so many trees that the Ringmaster could spend days looking for birds and still not have looked in every tree.

Anna glanced at the public library as she hurried by. For a second she thought of running in and seeing if Miss Petty, the librarian, could advise her. She realized she was scared. Why? What was there to be afraid of?

At the corner she turned left, being careful to pause long enough for the Ringmaster to catch up. She took a deep breath. The street was completely deserted. At the end of it lay the Grummer place, just beyond the crumbling stone wall. Could she convince the Ringmaster that the horses were there?

When she got to the wall, Anna stopped again to tie her shoe and listen. Three footsteps and then silence. Anna smiled as if she had a special secret. Then, taking a deep breath, she climbed over the stone wall and entered the forest.

Long ago all of this land had been the Grummer estate, with a big house and gardens. But everything was gone now, decayed and forgotten. The trees had grown close together, shutting out all the light. For a moment Anna felt too frightened to go on, but she thought of the horses and forced herself to put one foot in front of the next. The forest floor was littered with fallen branches and rotting tree trunks, and it was not easy to make her way through them.

She could hear the Ringmaster crashing through the trees behind her, swearing every now and then when he banged a shin or stubbed a toe. His breathing sounded hoarse and raspy. He wasn't trying to be quiet anymore. She wondered why.

This was the farthest Anna had ever ventured

into the woods. She skirted the broken foundation of the old house—all that was left of the Grummer place. That and a graveyard. With a shock Anna recognized six ancient gravestones leaning at odd angles, as if someone had deliberately pushed them over. They were dark with age, covered in moss, forgotten.

Anna was suddenly aware that she could no longer hear any sounds from the village, not even the church clock. She shuddered. And the Ringmaster had stopped tromping through the woods. Was he hiding behind a tree, watching her? Well, that was good, Anna thought, wasn't it? She wanted him to. She pulled herself together and continued with her charade.

She stopped and looked up into the already changing leaves. The maples were red, a startling, dripping kind of red against the blue of the sky. The oaks were turning rusty at the edges. The pines were green, as always, but dead pine needles covered the forest floor.

"Whooo wheet!" cried Anna, trying to make chirping noises. She held out her hand as if she had food in it. On and on she walked, looking up and shading her eyes as if to get a better view of the birds. "Whoo wheet! Come on out, little beauties," she called. "I know you're hiding in here!" Was it working? Would the Ringmaster believe her?

She paused to glance behind her. It was eerily quiet, so quiet that she could hear her breathing. She took another step, and another.

And then the ground disappeared beneath her feet.

WELL, WELL, WELL

At first Anna thought she had tripped on something. But she was falling, falling, and she kept on falling. It seemed like an eternity, but a few seconds later she landed in a shallow pool of water. For a minute she just sat there, wondering if she had broken anything. She felt under her. Deep pine needles lay beneath the water. She looked up. Thirty feet above her she could see the sky, a distant patch of blue.

She seemed to be sitting at the bottom of a well.

Yes, that must be it. It was an abandoned well. Over the years dead branches and pine needles must have hidden it.

Anna stood up. The sides of the well were narrow, smooth, and slippery. She felt around for a rope, a foothold, anything to help her out. There were only the straight walls, cold and damp and slick.

"Help!" she cried. "Help! Get me out of here!"

Suddenly the blue light from above dimmed and Anna saw a figure looking down at her. It was the Ringmaster, and he was grinning, a cigarette clenched between his teeth. "Say, girlie, you seem to be in a spot of trouble."

"Help!" said Anna. "Can you help me?"

"Well, now, that depends. Can you help *me*? I know you know what I'm looking for." He grinned grotesquely. "Them creatures."

Anna shivered. "I-I don't know what you're talking about."

"Ahh," said the Ringmaster. "It's just as well. Ha-ha—get it? Just as *well*? This secret is right for only one person." He pointed his thumb at his chest. "Me." He started to move away. "Bad luck, girlie," he called over his shoulder.

Anna stared up in disbelief. "But you can't leave me here!" she shouted.

The Ringmaster peered down into the well one last time. "Leave who where? Now that you have so kindly shown me where them flying things are, I can safely say I never seen you before in my life."

He turned away, and the long ash on his cigarette broke off and floated slowly down the well. Anna watched the ash glow for a second or two and then blow apart. She could hear the Ringmaster's feet crunching through the pine needles as he walked away.

"Help!" she cried. "Help me out of here!" But he did not come back, and there was no one else to hear her.

The patch of blue was growing dimmer—it was getting dark. Soon she would not be able to see anything. When would people start looking for her? How soon would people miss her?

And then a terrible thought struck her. *No one would miss her. No one would come looking for her.*

Aunt Formaldy might not be aware of Anna's absence for days, possibly even weeks. Why, Anna could disappear forever and Aunt Formaldy wouldn't notice.

Sam. Sam would look for her. But no, she was sick in bed. By the time she got better it might be too late.

A terrible get-me-out-of-here feeling closed in on Anna. The sides of the well were narrow and suffocating. She imagined them pressing in on her. She took a deep breath and screamed as loud as she could. Her scream echoed around the well, bouncing back at her over and over again.

Time passed. How much time Anna did not

know. It was getting colder, and she hugged herself.

I will never get out of this well, she thought. She closed her eyes. "ZYXWVUT—" she began.

And then a soft cooing sound interrupted her. She looked up. There was a fluttering and flapping, and suddenly Cyclone was balancing on Anna's knee.

He whinnied softly, slowly moving his wings back and forth. His gentle breath was warm and alive. She could hardly believe it.

"Cyclone," she said. "You came." She stroked his nose. Then she thought, *How can you rescue me?* She closed her eyes and made her hands into fists.

But Cyclone pawed her hand and she opened her eyes. He nudged her fist again, and as she opened it he dropped something into her palm.

A nutberry.

She turned it over in her hand. Cyclone whinnied. *Does he want me to eat this?* she wondered.

Never eat strange things, her mother had always said. But the horses eat them, Anna thought. So they can't be poisonous. Anyway, what difference would it make now?

And besides, she was hungry. One tiny nut couldn't hurt her.

Anna put the nutberry in her mouth. It had a strange sweet but bitter taste on her tongue. She bit into it. The shell was surprisingly easy to break. Inside, the center was soft. It tasted like lemons and melted in her mouth.

That's not so bad, she thought.

She was mistaken.

THE
PLUNGE

The stallion pawed the air impatiently and flew around Anna's head. She watched him sadly. *We are two lost creatures*, she said to herself, her eyes following Cyclone around and around.

Suddenly a fit of dizziness overcame her. It was from watching Cyclone fly in circles, she thought. But the dizziness turned into something else, something like a roller coaster ride called the Plunge, which Anna had tried once at the amusement park. Once had been enough. Now she felt as if she were falling again, falling fast and leaving her stomach behind.

It *was* poison, thought Anna, closing her eyes tight. Down and down she plunged, speeding through space. A high-pitched whining noise seemed to be coming from inside her head. "Is this what it feels like to die?" she asked out loud.

Suddenly she stopped falling. The whining noise stopped. It was deathly quiet.

Anna opened her eyes. She was sitting in a small boat of some kind, rocking gently in a pool of water. She stared at the boat in the dim light. A thick rope on top of it was tied into a neat bow. It had a familiar look to it. Nearby, a large hill rose out of the water.

She peered over the edge fearfully, wondering how deep the water was. It looked cold and nasty. She shivered violently.

It was then that Anna noticed her clothes had disappeared.

She looked at the boat, the rope, and the hill again. This was no boat, she realized. It was her shoe! That bow on top was the one she tied this morning. The pool she was floating in was the puddle of water at the bottom of the well. And the hill was the clothes she had just been wearing.

Now Anna was shivering so hard she could barely stand up. And it seemed to be getting colder by the minute.

"My socks, I have to find my socks," she muttered, bending down and reaching into the toe of her colossal shoe. Her teeth chattered and her hands shook with the cold. She dragged out a sock, which was now much bigger than she was. Anna sat down

in her shoe and worked at the hole in the toe of her
sock, making it bigger.

With stiff fingers she pulled out the lace of her
shoe. It was long and heavy. The pointed end felt as
sharp and strong as a screwdriver, and Anna used it
to poke two more holes in the sock. Then she slipped
the sock over her head.

It fit her like a dress, though it came down way
past her toes. She stuck her arms through the holes
she had just made, untied the shoelace, and wound it
around her waist. She breathed a sigh of relief. Although the sock was damp at one end, it was thick
and soft and felt like a warm coat. Her shaking
stopped.

At that moment Anna felt a rush of wind over
her head. A piercing cry shattered the silence. She
looked up and nearly fainted dead away.

Suspended in the air above her was the most
frightening thing Anna had ever seen. A wild stallion
pawed the air. He was immense, so white he was almost blue. When he reared up on his hind legs, his
flanks flashed in the dim light from above. Suddenly
he was in front of her, and Anna saw his wings, great
white wings spreading out like an angel's.

It was Cyclone. But he was big and powerful and
terrifying now, not the tiny little stallion of a few

minutes ago. He whinnied again, and his whinny was like a battle cry, commanding and urgent. What had happened to him? How did he get so big?

No. That was not the question, Anna knew. The question was, How did she get so *small*?

Now Cyclone settled at the bottom of the well, right next to Anna's shoe, snorting and stamping. He tossed his head impatiently. Anna looked at him, and he stared steadily back at her. He nudged her, his nostrils exhaling warm air, and suddenly she stopped being afraid. He was Cyclone, and, big or small, she knew she trusted him.

She looked up at the faraway darkening sky and then back at the narrow and slippery walls of the well. She took a deep breath and hitched up her sock-dress. Lacing her fingers into the stallion's mane, she pulled herself onto his back and buried her face in his neck. His body was warm and strong. Anna's heart pounded so hard she thought it might burst right out of her chest. Something told her she was about to have the ride of her life.

In less time than it took to fall into the well she was out of it. Like a shot the stallion darted up into the sky and over the treetops, with Anna hanging on for dear life. After a moment he slowed, stretched his wings, and soared smoothly over the village. Hugging Cyclone's neck as tightly as she could, Anna raised her head and looked around her.

She gasped. In the west, a last glimmer of light touched the horizon. To the east, a giant round moon floated up like a hot-air balloon. And below lay the village of Greeley, its winding streets and neat houses bathed in moonlight. Beaver Brook glinted in the dark, a flash of silver. The Grummer place, with the well she had just escaped from, was hidden among the trees.

Everything was beautiful and serene. Below her the world twinkled like a jewel. Anna felt the soft night air blow through her hair. The stallion's powerful body was warm. She hugged Cyclone tight and exhaled. She was safe.

It could be a dream, the one she sometimes had of flying over treetops, but Anna knew it wasn't. This was real. And whatever happened, nothing could change this moment.

The stallion snorted and wheeled smoothly through the night sky. Anna could feel the muscles in his neck as he moved his wings. His mane, as white as the rest of him, streamed out behind him, caressing Anna's cheek. She leaned forward and hugged Cyclone tighter. She could feel him twitch slightly under her fingers, as if he were answering her.

She could make out her school, GERMS, now,

right by the power lines. How different it looked from up here. She thought of her classmates and how shocked they would be if they could see her. They would stare, mouths hanging open. Stacy would say, "Oooh, that looks so *dangerous*!" Noah would say, "Awesome!" Walker—Anna winced when she thought of what Walker would say: "Wait until my uncle hears about this!"

Beyond the school lay Mrs. Perry's field, dark like a stain. Anna wondered if there were still circus people down there, hiding, all their lights out, waiting for the police to try to throw them out.

Suddenly, from the field, a shard of white light pierced the night sky. It arced upward and moved slowly across the blackness toward the stallion and Anna. Another blade of light joined it, sweeping through the dark. Searchlights! Anna's heart skipped a beat. She was certain she knew who was down there and what he was looking for. "Hurry!" she cried out to Cyclone. "It's coming our way!" The light was close now, almost blinding Anna. "He'll see us!"

The stallion seemed to understand. Just as the powerful beam was about to surround them, he stretched his neck out and pressed his wings behind him.

In a flash they were beyond the reach of the

lights, Anna scarcely knew how. One minute they were gliding quietly over the village, the next minute they were shooting across the sky like a comet.

Once again Cyclone slowed and circled. Now they were so high up Anna could see the next village and the one next to that. Boosic Lake glinted dully below like a metal mirror. In the distance Anna could see the dark outline of Mount Monadnock. The searchlights looked feeble from up here, far away and unimportant.

But it was cold and getting colder. A cold numbness was beginning to spread through her body in spite of the warm stallion beneath her.

"Home," she whispered to Cyclone regretfully. She squeezed her legs together and gave his mane a little tug. Maybe he would understand.

He seemed to.

With a single powerful movement of his wings he plunged down, with Anna holding fast. "Oh!" she cried. The wind roared in her ears and stung her eyes, and she pressed her face into the stallion's powerful neck. They hurtled through the air, and in seconds Anna found herself crashing through leaves, scattering nutberries and twigs. Suddenly they stopped moving. She opened her eyes.

They were in her tree. At least, it looked like her tree, except it was huge.

Anna dismounted from Cyclone. Her knees trembled violently. She had to sit down. The branches of the tree were as wide as a highway. She looked up. The rest of the horses hovered overhead. They were big now, and Anna could feel the wind from their wings.

She sat and looked around her. Even the leaves were larger than she was. Everything was. Her book lay on a wide branch, open. She got up carefully and walked over to it. It was as big as a table, too big to pick up now. A half-filled glass of milk stood near it, like a pillar. An enormous empty plate held crumbs that now looked almost as big as full-sized cookies.

Anna went over to the stairs and peered down. There was no climbing down those. They were stairs for a giant, each step impossibly far away. It was like standing on a cliff. Anna looked down and up. The other branches were distant and unreachable. There seemed to be no way out of her tree.

But of course there was. Cyclone. She would ride the stallion and get help.

Help? Anna sat down again. Who was going to help her and these lost creatures? The FBI? The army? Aunt Formaldy?

Sam. Even if Sam couldn't help, she was a friend.

And at that moment Anna badly needed one.

WAKE UP!

Sam was sound asleep. Peering through the window, Anna could hear her breathing deeply.

"Sam! Wake up! Over here! Open up!" Sam turned over and opened her eyes.

"Sam! The window! Open the window!"

Sam turned on the light and looked around her. "Anna? Is that you? Where are you?"

"Over here, outside your window. Hurry up!"

Sam jumped out of bed and hurried to the window. She peered out, pressing her nose against the screen. "I can't see you," she said, raising the screen.

Anna stepped onto the windowsill.

"Oh boy," Sam said, and got back in bed, pulling the covers up and closing her eyes.

"Sam!" Anna cried.

Sam opened an eye. "Shhh. I'm dreaming. I must have a fever." She rolled over.

"You're not dreaming, Sam. It's me. Wake up. You've got to help me."

Sam turned over and looked back at the windowsill. Anna was sitting down now, her little legs dangling over the edge. Sam rubbed her eyes and shook her head. "Anna. Please," she said, getting out of bed and cautiously approaching her friend. "I'm dreaming. Right?"

"No, no. I can explain. Sort of," Anna said.

"Your voice sounds funny. You're squeaking."

"I am?" Anna cleared her throat. "Could you get me down from here?"

"How?" Sam said. "You mean *carry* you?"

"We have to be calm," Anna said.

"I *am* calm," protested Sam. "I am always calm." She held out her hands. "See? Calm."

Anna nodded, and stepped into Sam's hands. "Don't squeeze me or drop me, whatever you do," she warned.

Sam said nothing, concentrating as she walked carefully over to the bed. Anna stepped out of her hands and stumbled over a wrinkle in the blanket.

Sam knelt on the floor next to the bed so she could be level with Anna. For a minute the two girls just stared at each other.

"What happened?" Sam said finally.

Knowing her voice was small, too, Anna tried

hard to speak up. "Remember those strange birds right after the hurricane?"

Sam nodded.

"They aren't birds," Anna said.

"Not birds," repeated Sam.

"They're—no, wait," Anna interrupted herself. "Look out on the windowsill."

Sam looked out. "There's nothing here," she said.

"Oh. He must have gone back." Anna was disappointed, but she was relieved, too. Cyclone was much safer in her tree than outside, where anyone could see him.

"Gone back. Who must have gone back?" asked Sam. She knelt by the bed again. "Someone was on my *windowsill*?"

"Some*thing*," corrected Anna. She climbed onto Sam's pillow so she could be closer to Sam's face, and then she told her everything.

"When I got to the tree and realized how small I was, I decided to come here for help . . ." Anna finally said, her voice trailing off at the end. What, after all, could Sam do to help her?

For a long time Sam was silent. She studied Anna, who was so tiny she barely made a dent in the pillow. She was like a doll, her face as small as a daisy.

"I don't know what to do," Anna finally said.

Sam drummed her fingers on the bed. "We'll think of something," she said at last. She considered Anna. "Are you like that for good?"

"Like . . . ?" Anna didn't understand at first. Then she gasped. "Like this *for good*?" She hadn't thought about being this size *forever*! Too much had happened, too much kept happening, for her to think about the future.

Forever! "I . . . I don't know," she answered. "Oh, Sam. What will happen to me?"

Maybe I'll end up in the circus, thought Anna. What would they do with her? Would they put her in a cage? Crowds of people coming to look at her, gaping mouths, Aunt Formaldy saying, "No, no, that is certainly not my dear niece."

"What's that you're wearing?" Sam asked suddenly.

"A sock," said Anna, looking down at herself. "Speaking of socks," she said, bending down to rub her cold feet, "I wish I had some."

"Of course!" exclaimed Sam.

Anna watched curiously as her friend opened the closet door and reached up to a shelf. She lifted down a small green trunk. Anna recognized it immediately because she had one just like it.

It was filled with Suzy clothes. Doll clothes.

Sam opened the box and said, "Help yourself. You might want to change your . . . your clothes. Not that that old sock isn't fine," she hastened to add.

Anna looked at the choices before her. There were party dresses, slacks, jeans, sweaters, shirts, shoes, boots, jackets, all designed for Suzy. Anna had owned the same clothes for her Suzy doll, but she hadn't taken nearly such good care of hers. Sam had not only shoes but matching socks. Anna's doll clothes had been lost long ago.

Sam was back in her closet, looking for something, while Anna picked out brown pants and a blue sweater and put them on. To her surprise, they fit almost perfectly. The blue sweater was a wee bit long and she turned up the sleeves. She peered into the clothes trunk again. It was big enough to climb into, and she did. She opened the drawer on the left and found a pair of blue socks.

"Ahhh, that's better!" said Anna, wiggling her toes inside the warm socks.

Sam turned off the light in the closet and came back to the bed. "Anna?" she said. "Where are you?"

Anna popped her head out of the trunk. "I'm here, helping myself to socks."

Sam stared at her. "You look like a Suzy doll," she said.

"Can I see?" asked Anna.

Sam reached for a small mirror on her desk and held it in front of Anna, who had climbed out of the trunk.

Anna gazed at herself for a minute. "I look like a regular girl," she said, relieved.

Sam didn't say anything. She was holding a box, and now she set it gently on the bed.

"What's that?" Anna asked.

"It will take only a few minutes to assemble it, I think," said Sam by way of an answer. She opened the box and pulled out a large assortment of wood and plastic pieces. Anna watched as she snapped the pieces together.

"There," said Sam, standing back to look at her handiwork.

It was a dollhouse, the one Anna had secretly hoped for on Christmas several years before but hadn't mentioned to anyone. She had forgotten all about it until now. "It's the Suzy House," she said, her eyes wide. It was a dream house—blue with yellow shutters and a yellow door, two stories tall, with a chimney. Silk flowers spilled out of little window boxes.

"Wait a second," Sam said. She opened another

box and pulled out a bed, sofas, chairs, tables, and even a bathtub. Anna watched Sam's large hands open the front of the house and arrange the pieces of furniture inside. "It's all yours," she said, lifting the house off the bed and setting it on the floor.

"Won't your aunt wonder where you are?" asked Sam. She was lying on the floor on her stomach, looking at Anna, who was sitting in a little rocking chair on the porch of the dollhouse.

Anna shook her head. "Hardly. She forgets that I live in the house except when she sees me."

Sam got a funny look on her face. "Isn't there *anyone* who cares for you?" she asked earnestly. "No nanny? No housekeeper? No anyone?"

"I'm getting used to it," Anna said. "Sort of."

"It must feel awful," Sam said, frowning. "But I guess it's a good thing under the circumstances." She peered at the small figure before her. "It would be pretty bad if your aunt found out about this."

"If I miss school they'll call her, though."

"I was forgetting about that," said Sam. "Well, at least we have tomorrow to figure things out. It's lucky we don't have school."

"What about your parents? Didn't they come yesterday?" asked Anna.

Sam had leaned over to put on her slippers. "They couldn't make it," she said, her voice suddenly subdued. "They said next week for sure they'll be here." She stared at her slippers for a few moments. Then she looked up and grinned. "Right now we've got more important things to think about, like finding an antidote for your . . . size."

"Can we start thinking tomorrow?" asked Anna, yawning. She suddenly felt too weary to do anything but lie down. "I'm so tired."

"You'll need a blanket," said Sam. She left the room and came back with a washcloth.

Anna dragged the washcloth into the dollhouse and climbed in the bed, snuggling under her warm blanket. "We'll figure everything out tomorrow," she heard Sam say, and then she fell fast asleep.

IT CAN'T BE
JUST A
COINCIDENCE

The smell of bacon woke Anna up. She stretched and yawned and opened her eyes, wondering if her mom and dad had saved some for her. She looked around. She was in a strange bed in a strange room. And then she remembered just how strange! She jumped out of bed and looked through the dollhouse window into Sam's room. Sam was nowhere to be seen.

Hurrying downstairs, Anna stepped out onto the porch of the dollhouse and stopped in surprise. There on the little round table was a doll's plate, and on it were servings of hot scrambled eggs and bacon. Next to it was a teacup filled with orange juice. She sat down and took a drink.

The door opened and Sam walked in. "Hi," she said casually, as if everything were normal and Anna weren't just eight inches high.

"Thanks for the breakfast," said Anna. She took a bite of bacon.

"Mrs. Birkenhead made it," Sam said. She walked to her closet and pulled out a sweatshirt. "She said it's going to be cold," she added, pulling it over her head. And then, looking down at herself, she asked, "Is this yours?"

Anna looked up at the faded red sweatshirt. It was the one she had lent Sam the other day. "I guess so. But you can wear it."

Sam pulled a crumpled piece of paper out of the sweatshirt pocket and squinted at the writing. "This is that paper we found in the box in your barn."

"Let me see," said Anna, getting up from her rocking chair.

Sam got down on her hands and knees and spread the paper on the floor. Anna walked over and looked down at it curiously. She recognized the handwriting immediately.

"It's those biology notes," she murmured. She stepped onto the paper now and walked along the words, trying to make out her father's handwriting again. "Oh yes—hereditary variability . . . speciation . . . isolation . . . reductive properties . . ." She peered hard at a word. "What's this? It looks like 'Eolippus'—something like that."

Sam leaned forward and peered at the writing.

"No, I think that's an *h*. Eohippus. What's that?"

She went over to her bookshelf, pulled out a book, and laid it on the floor next to Anna. "Eohippus," she said, flipping the pages. "Here it is. 'Eohippus, or "dawn horse," ' " she read out loud, " 'was an early ancestor of the modern horse. It lived 50 million years ago and was only ten inches high . . .' " She stopped reading and looked over at Anna, whose mouth was open in amazement.

"Ten inches high," repeated Anna.

They stared at each other.

Anna walked around the paper, peering down at the large words. "It can't just be a coincidence, can it?"

Sam shook her head. "Doesn't sound like it."

"See, look," said Anna, pointing at the words with her feet, "all these words, like 'hereditary variability' and 'reductive properties' and 'speciation'—those must be about the horses. I'm sure they are—they're biology words, explaining about them."

Sam was nodding her head slowly. " 'Reductive,' " she said, "like in 'reduce,' the way if you go on a diet you reduce." She knelt down to get closer to Anna and said pointedly, "You get smaller."

"Like me!" Anna exclaimed.

"I wonder what else we could find out if we had that box," Sam said.

With a start, Anna realized what Sam was talking about. "You mean there might be something else in there about the horses—"

"And being small."

Anna's heart skipped a beat. Was a solution to her smallness in the box? "I've looked everywhere for it," she said. "Every time Aunt Formaldy was out I looked. I didn't miss a single room." A note of desperation had entered her small voice.

"Did you think?" Sam said.

"Think?"

"Yeah. As in 'Sit down, close your eyes, and think.' That's what Mrs. Birkenhead always tells me to do when I lose something. Think from the moment your aunt saw you with it—what day was it?"

"Thursday," said Anna.

"Okay, think about Thursday."

Anna looked doubtful but closed her eyes anyway and concentrated. She thought about finding the box with Sam and how exciting it was. She remembered how her aunt had looked when she took the box from her, the disgust on her face. She heard her say, 'I will dispose of that,' and the retreating footsteps, the muffled noise in the background. Nothing came to mind. She opened her eyes and looked at Sam. "You've still got a cobweb on your sweatshirt," she remarked, reaching up and trying to pull it off with her little hands.

And then it came to her. Her aunt's face. It was filled with disgust because the box was covered in cobwebs and dust.

"She didn't hide the box," Anna said slowly, "she threw it away!" She jumped up. "What time is it?"

"A quarter to eight."

"We have to hurry! It's Tuesday—garbage day. And the garbage men usually get to my house around nine."

NOW YOU SEE IT,
NOW YOU DON'T

What if she sees me?" whispered Sam, tiptoeing across Anna's backyard.

"It's okay. You're wearing my sweatshirt. Maybe
she'll think you're me. She never seems to recognize
me anyway." Anna peered out of the top of Sam's
pocket. She was holding on with both hands, even
though she knew Sam would be careful not to bend
over and tip her out. Still, it was a bumpy ride.

"The garbage cans are just outside the back door,
in that little shed," said Anna, pointing her tiny finger.

Sam walked swiftly to the shed and opened the
door. There were three garbage cans.

"Well, here goes," she said, reaching over to
the one on the left and lifting the lid. It slipped out
of her hand and crashed onto the cement floor.
"Oops."

Anna held on tight while Sam bent down to pick it up. "Just a plastic bag," Anna noted with disappointment.

Sam replaced the lid and opened the second can. And there was the box, right on top, shoved down onto empty milk cartons and cereal boxes. Anna stared at the red roses glinting in the morning light. Would the answers to her questions be inside?

Suddenly a loud voice interrupted Anna's thoughts. "What, may I ask, are you doing?" It was Aunt Formaldy. She was leaning out of her bedroom window, a little cap perched jauntily at an angle on her head, her diamond earrings flashing in the sunlight. She looked dressed to go out.

Anna ducked down into Sam's pocket, her heart pounding. Had her aunt seen her? "I'm just throwing something away," Anna heard Sam say. She could hear Sam putting the garbage lid back.

"Shouldn't you be in school?"

"It's teachers' conference day," Sam said.

"Well, then, you will probably want to study in your room."

Sam hesitated.

"*Now.*"

Anna felt Sam move away from the garbage cans. She heard the bedroom window slam shut. "She's watching me," Sam said in a low voice. "She thinks I'm you. I'll just go upstairs until she leaves."

Anna could tell Sam was going into the house and upstairs. In a moment Sam spoke. "You can come out now."

Anna popped her head out of Sam's pocket. They were in Anna's room. "We have to get back down there," she said. "Before the garbage men get here."

Sam nodded. "Let's wait a minute and then see if she's gone. It looked like she had her coat on." She walked over to the door and they both listened. Sure enough, Aunt Formaldy's footsteps passed Anna's room and they could hear her going down the stairs. The door opened and closed. She had left the house.

But as the girls listened for further sounds there was a sudden banging and crashing.

"She sure is making a commotion out there," said Sam.

Anna strained her little ears to hear. "That's not Aunt Formaldy!" she cried. "It's the garbage men! Oh, hurry, Sam. We have to get that box!"

But by the time they got there, the garbage can was empty. All that remained was a squashed banana peel and two shriveled beans. The box was gone. And so were any answers that might have been in it.

Despair washed over Anna. Would she have to live the rest of her life as a Suzy doll? Too terrible! She just wouldn't think of it. "ZYX," she said through clenched teeth, "WVUT . . ."

Then she stopped. A wild plan had begun to form in her mind. And it frightened her half to death.

A DARING
PLAN

I have an idea," said Anna. From where she stood she had a good view of Sam's chin, but that was all.

"Good," said Sam. "I don't."

"Let's go talk about it in my tree. I have to check on H-Rose."

Sam looked down at Anna in her pocket. "Do you think the horses will be there right now?"

"I hope so."

Anna hung on while Sam went back upstairs to Anna's room and stepped out into the tree. "I don't see anything," Sam said, looking around.

An agitated cooing and fluttering could be heard in the upper branches. "Here, help me get out," Anna said. "When they see me, they'll know it's all right."

Sam reached into her pocket and set Anna down carefully on the yellow sofa. Suddenly Cyclone was over their heads, beating his wings furiously and glaring at Sam. Then he plunged down to the sofa and stood beside Anna protectively.

Sam gasped. "It's really true," she whispered, not taking her eyes off the tiny winged stallion. "I believed you, but . . . but . . ." She didn't finish what she was saying. Instead she reached behind her, felt a chair, and sat down.

"I'll be back in a while," said Anna, worrying about H-Rose. She had not changed his bandage since yesterday after school, just before she fell in the well. Sam nodded, too thunderstruck to reply.

Anna climbed onto Cyclone's back and gave his mane a gentle tug. They rose to the top of the tree.

The little colt was still lying there in his nest, his eyes closed. Anna jumped off Cyclone's back, holding her breath. "Please be better," she whispered.

She bent down to feel his head and let her breath out. He was a little cooler than before, she was almost positive.

She gave him water and changed his bandage. This was much harder to do now that she was small, and Beauty, the mother, hovered about anxiously while Anna struggled with the gauze. At last she had

H-Rose clean. Gently, she leaned over and kissed his face. "You're going to be just fine," she said, hoping she sounded more confident than she felt. He opened his eyes briefly and shut them again.

When Anna returned to Sam, she found her still sitting on the chair, her eyes wide with amazement. She had her hand out, and the mischievous black colt with the white blaze was standing on it, eating a nutberry.

"I think he likes me," Sam said in a hushed voice. "Does he have a name?"

"Not yet," said Anna. "Any ideas?"

"How about Imp?" As Sam said that, Imp flew up to the overhanging branch and dropped a nutberry on Sam's head. She laughed. "Yeah, I think that name is just about right."

"I have an idea about getting the box," said Anna.

Her friend looked at her with interest. "Let's hear it," she said.

Anna opened her mouth to explain and then stopped for a minute. Her idea suddenly seemed crazy and dangerous. But maybe that's exactly what was needed—a crazy, dangerous plan. She made herself comfortable on the arm of the chair and began.

THE
SEARCH

Ssst! It's me!" Anna scratched at the window
screen and peered into Sam's room. It was late and
the house was quiet.

"Hi," said Sam, jumping out of her bed and
pulling up the screen. She was dressed in black—
black pants, black jacket, black ski cap.

Anna hesitated for a moment. "I hope it's okay
to bring a horse in here," she said as she swooped
through the open window and down to the floor.

"I left my bike under the bushes. Meet you out
front," Sam whispered, carefully opening the bedroom door.

Sam pedaled down the street and Anna followed
on Cyclone, a few feet over Sam's head. The moon
had a hazy ring around it but shed enough light so
that Anna could make out the sleeping houses and
the empty streets. *Are we the only people awake in Gree-*

ley? she wondered as a church bell sounded the quarter hour, a single clear note that hung in the cold air. Far away a truck rumbled along a highway. The eerie cry of a loon drifted up from Boosic Lake. Otherwise, there was not a sound.

"We're almost there!" Anna said encouragingly as Sam pedaled furiously up the hill that led to the dump.

Sam looked over her shoulder at Anna. "That's easy for you to say," she replied, panting.

Anna and her father used to go to the dump together every Saturday morning. Everyone went to the dump on Saturday morning. If you wanted to see your neighbors, this was the place to hang out. Aunt Formaldy, of course, would not dream of even driving past the dump, and one of the first things she had done when she moved to the Farrington house was order a weekly garbage pickup service.

But Anna had never seen the dump from above, and her heart sank when they reached it. It was much, much larger than she had thought; piles of garbage rose into the sky like mountains. She and Cyclone swooped low over them, her hopes of finding the box diminishing rapidly. They flew over to Sam, who was getting off her bike and looking around her in dismay.

"Pee-yu," Sam said.

There was a small mountain of refrigerators and washing machines and computers, another of plastic and glass bottles, and the one that smelled so bad, a huge one of everything imaginable—food, moldy rags, cat litter. How would they ever find an old box in this mess? A colossal bulldozer sat silent next to the smelly pile. By tomorrow all of this would be flattened into bits.

"I . . . I think I'll start looking at the far end and . . . just keep looking," Anna said to Sam, without much hope. She urged Cyclone over to the largest pile and peered down at beef bones and broken plates. Cyclone whinnied as if in sympathy. She hugged his neck and whispered, "It's all right, Cyclone. We'll figure this out." But how would they? The box, if it was here, was surely buried.

Anna and Cyclone flew low over the garbage pile, trying to see every inch of it.

After an hour Anna had examined most of the pile. She shivered. The night air was getting colder and damper by the minute. "Any luck?" she asked Sam, who was wandering along the outskirts of the pile, kicking at the edges, looking defeated. Sam shook her head. "Me neither," said Anna. "I guess it's hopeless. I'm just going to check the side of the pile where the bulldozer is. I'll be right back."

She and Cyclone swooped up across the pile and down to the far side. Each fish head, each half-eaten hamburger, was grotesquely huge, repulsive beyond words. Anna wondered if she would ever want to eat again. Some of the garbage had already been flattened beyond recognition, but Anna peered down at the pile in front of the bulldozer.

A glint caught her eye. Flying closer, she squinted at something familiar. It was lying on the ground tilted on its side—a red rose just visible in the moonlight.

By the time the girls returned to Sam's house, it was well after midnight.

"Phew!" Sam whispered, setting the bag with the precious box down on the bed in her room.

Cyclone had flown back to the Justin Case tree, and Anna was sitting in the little rocking chair, rocking back and forth impatiently. "Hurry, let's look in the box," she said.

Sam picked up the bag, slipped the box out, and set it on the floor in front of Anna. "Here goes," she said, lifting the lid.

Suddenly there was a knock at the door. Sam let the lid fall and jumped up. "Hide!" she hissed. Anna hurried into the dollhouse just as Sam's door opened.

"Hi, Mrs. Birkenhead," Anna heard Sam say.

"What are you doing up at this time of night, Sam?" a sleepy voice replied. "Did you have a bad dream?"

"It's okay, Mrs. Birkenhead," came Sam's voice. "I . . . I guess I'm just hungry."

"Well, dear, that's fine. I'm glad you have your appetite back. I'll just run down and get you a wee snack, but then I think you need to turn off the lights and go back to sleep."

"Thanks, Mrs. Birkenhead. I will, I promise," Sam said.

In a few moments Anna heard Mrs. Birkenhead return. "Here's a nice little plate of bread and cheese, my dear. And a cup of warm milk." Sam thanked her, sounding genuinely grateful. Then Anna heard the door close softly.

"That was close," whispered Sam, chewing on a piece of bread. "You can come out now, but be quiet."

Anna peeked out the front door of the dollhouse. "I can't *be* noisy. I'm too small."

Politely setting the plate on the floor within Anna's reach, Sam poured a small amount of the milk into a tiny teacup. Then she tiptoed over to the box.

Anna bent down to the plate and ate a bit of cheese. Then, after taking a few sips of the warm milk, she pulled off a tiny piece of bread and chewed it absent-mindedly as she stood on tiptoes, trying to see in the box. "Do you think we'll find the antidote?" she asked eagerly. "I'm getting tired of being sma—" She jumped back and put her hands to her head. "I don't feel so good," she said. "Ohhhh, I really feel strange."

Sam looked down at Anna in amazement. "Anna!"

Anna could just make out Sam's voice, but it sounded as if it were coming from a long distance, through water and fog and brick walls. She felt herself being tossed up into the air, like a beach ball. "Help," she tried to say, but it came out "HoooooooooooooooP!" She heard a loud whooshing sound in her ears, and her head felt as though it would pop.

Suddenly the tossing and bouncing and whooshing stopped.

"You're back!" announced Sam, who had jumped up from the floor and was gazing at Anna in disbelief.

And it was true. She was. She was her normal size again, standing in the middle of the floor. "Um, do you have some clothes I could borrow?"

Sam was already on her way to the closet and came back with jeans and a shirt. "You sure looked strange—almost as if you were exploding."

Anna pulled on the clothes and ran over to the mirror on the wall to look at herself. "I look the same," she said. "I'm the same old me! Here, stand next to me. See? We're the same size!" Anna jumped up on Sam's bed and took a flying leap off. "I'm meeeeee!"

"Do you think it was something you did?"

Anna shook her head. "I didn't do anything. I was just standing there, eating cheese and bread."

"Just standing there, eating cheese and bread," Sam repeated thoughtfully. Suddenly both girls burst out laughing, as if that were the funniest thing they had ever heard. "I didn't do anything," said Sam between shrieks of laughter. "I was just standing there, eating cheese and bread."

Anna rolled on the floor, holding her stomach, she was laughing so hard. "Eating cheese and bread!" she gasped.

There was a knock at the door. "Oops," said Sam. She looked around. "Closet," she whispered. Anna slipped into the closet just as Sam's door opened.

"Really, Sam." Mrs. Birkenhead's voice sounded tired and worried. "What has come over you?"

"I'm sorry, Mrs. B. I really am. I was just sitting here, eating cheese and bread." Anna, in the closet, held both hands over her mouth, stifling her laughter.

"Well, I think that's enough for now, dear." Anna could hear footsteps. "Hmmm, you do feel a little feverish still. Now hop in bed, there's a good girl. You don't want to get sick all over again."

It was several minutes before Anna heard the door close again.

"I better leave," Anna whispered, tiptoeing out of the closet and seeing that the light was off. "We can look at everything in the box tomorrow." Suddenly her future was looking a lot brighter, now that she was her normal size.

Sam agreed. "She's such a worrywart. She'll be fretting all night about me."

"That's nice," replied Anna.

"Yeah," Sam said, sounding surprised. "It is."

NOTHING EXCITING EVER HAPPENS AROUND HERE

Anna's alarm went off the next morning long before she was ready to wake up. She breathed a sigh of relief when she saw that she was still dressed in her pajamas and still just the right size for her bed. Could she have dreamed everything? Were the horses part of the dream?

She hurried out the window and into her tree. All of the tiny horses were there, calmly eating nutberries and drinking the water Anna had poured out for them before she went to bed, but when she rushed up the stairs to check on H-Rose, he was gone. She closed her eyes and took a deep breath. *Maybe he fell out of the nest*, she thought. *Maybe he's lying below somewhere, injured—or dead.*

She ran down the stairs, stopping at each branch to look for him, but he was nowhere to be seen.

"H-Rose!" she cried. "H-Rose!"

A small whinnying sound came from above. Anna looked up. And there he was, balancing on the branch overhead, his wings fluttering back and forth feebly. Anna could have sworn he looked proud of himself. Beauty, his mother, hovered over him. H-Rose floated clumsily down to Anna's shoulder and nibbled her ear.

"H-Rose," she whispered, gently lifting him and holding him in her hand. The bandage still clung to him, but it was white. No sign of blood. His eyes were clear, and as she stroked his nose she could tell that the fever was gone.

"My uncle is looking for butterflies," announced Walker at recess that morning. It was raining, and all the students were in the classroom.

Anna and Sam exchanged glances.

"Yeah, he sleeps all day and spends his nights at that old Grummer place," Walker went on. "They're *nocturnal* butterflies, he says." He gave Anna a sidelong look. "He's not the only one who has seen them, he says."

"Is that why he's still here?" asked Avery.

"He's still here because he feels like it," snapped Walker. "He does what he wants. Did you hear about Monday night?"

"My mom was involved," Avery said proudly.

Neighbors had complained to the police about

the searchlights. Officer Mile had hurried to the Perry field, his siren blaring.

"I didn't hear any siren," Noah said.

"That's because your ears are so small," Walker explained. "That's why we call you 'No-ear.' " In fact, Noah's ears *were* pretty small.

"The police told my uncle to *cease and desist*," Walker continued, "and you know what he told them?" Walker paused dramatically. "He said they had to get a court order!" He was beaming. "What a guy."

"Was there a gun battle or anything?" Noah asked.

"Well, no, not yet," Walker answered. "You have to do these things legal-like to begin with. My uncle says he does this stuff all the time."

"No gun battle," said Noah, turning away. "Nothing exciting ever happens around here."

Anna did not even need to look at Sam to know that she was trying to hide a smile.

The day ticked by slowly. All Anna could think about was the horses and the box. Would the horses be safe? Would the box give a clue about where they were from or how her father had seemed to know about them?

By the end of the day, she was so anxious that when the school bell finally rang she almost jumped out of her skin.

"What's that car doing?" Sam said. The girls had left the school together and were hurrying to Anna's house. Sam nodded in the direction of a beat-up old car that was moving slowly past them in the rain.

Anna gave the car a sidelong glance. The windows were steamed up and she couldn't see the driver, but she didn't have to. Something told her it was the Ringmaster. "Pretend you don't see him," Anna said, looking straight ahead.

"It's the Ringmaster, isn't it?" said Sam. "Do you think he's surprised to see you're alive?"

Anna nodded grimly. "And maybe disappointed."

The car sped up and disappeared around the corner, but not before they caught a glimpse of Walker leaning out one of the windows, looking back at them.

"Well, they're gone," said Sam, letting her breath out.

"For now," Anna replied.

Anna's house was empty when the girls got there, after stopping first at Sam's to retrieve the box. They hurried up the stairs to Anna's room and stepped out into the tree.

The strange black box was battered from its dump experience, but the red roses shone brightly and the mother-of-pearl glistened. Anna opened it carefully and picked up the diary.

It smelled old, like dry leaves. She noticed that her hand was shaking.

She read:

Diary 1771
Lucinda Anna Farrington

I dare not tell anyone, not even Jeb, for surely he will think me bewitched. I write this only to you, dear Diary, and perhaps to some One in the Future who will read this and learn of these passing strange Events.

I was but thirteen years of age when a violent Storm blew for two days over my home in Virginia. The Storm passed at last, and as early dawn broke I arose and witnessed Devastation everywhere— trees had been knocked flat as if by some giant Hand, roofs had been torn off houses and barns, and pigs had been tossed from pen to pasture. The Orchard where I had played every day was gone except for one Tree. I sat *beneath this Tree for a long time and wept.*

Soon I became aware of a strange sound, a small Whinnying, as of a Horse. Unless my ears deceived me, it came from the branches of the Tree above me! I climbed up, and there I saw a Sight that to this very day fills me with Awe and Wonder. Hovering just over my head was a small Flock of Winged Horses!

Anna stopped reading for a second and looked at Sam. "Winged horses!" they both exclaimed.
Anna continued:

I had heard stories of diminutive flying Horses at my mother's knee, just as she had heard them from her mother, who had heard them from hers. There was, according to the Legend, a small and mysterious Island but one hundred miles due east of the Islands of Assateague and Chincoteague.

This mysterious Island was called Pegasuteague and was covered at all times by a Mist or Fog which seemed to settle over it like a Veil. According to the Legend, there were fabulous Trees on the Island, Trees of great Size which never lost their Leaves and which produced a strange fruit called the Nutberry.

"Nutberries!" cried Anna. "Those must be Justin Case trees!" She read on:

These Winged Creatures were supposed to reside in the great trees and live off the Nutberries. It was said that the Nutberries themselves had a special power to make that which is Large, Small.

The trees, the Stories said, were the Protectors of the Creatures, broad and strong enough to withstand the terrible Storms that plague that Part of the Atlantic Ocean.

I had always believed these stories to be just that—stories. Until now.

The Horses I beheld were frightened, and I sat quite still so as not to frighten them more. At last, one of the Creatures, a beautiful golden Stallion, alit on the branch directly in front of me and placed before me an Acorn, or so I thought it was, which he apparently had held in his mouth.

At that moment I heard my mother calling for me and I quickly put the Acorn in my apron pocket and climbed down the tree and ran to the house. As soon as I was able I returned to the Orchard and climbed up the lone Tree. But the Creatures were gone.

When I told Mother what I had beheld in that Orchard, she felt my forehead and put me to bed for three days. I never mentioned the Creatures again.

But I saved that acorn. Years later, when Jeb and I had married and had moved to New Hampshire, I planted it outside our window. It has grown into a fine tree which has become the Talk of the Town, for it is of surpassing Beauty and Strangeness. It is never bare, but is always covered in large pear-shaped leaves. It bears a multitude of Nutberries, but not one has ever taken root and grown.

I look for storms eagerly, but here in New Hampshire they are middling and local. Still, I continue to hope that someday a Cyclone will bring the Horses to my Tree, which waits here for them, Just In Case.

THE DOTTED LINE

Justin Case," Anna whispered. "*Just In Case!* She planted this tree *just in case* the horses came back to her." Anna shook her head in disbelief. "And they did. That is, they came back to *me*."

Sam's eyes were wide with wonder. "It's as if she hoped you would come along and read this someday. You're the 'some One in the Future.' "

"It's all so strange!" Anna said.

Suddenly Imp, who had been dropping nutberries onto Sam's head every few minutes, lost his balance and tumbled into Sam's lap. "What a clown you are," Sam said, laughing. She looked up at Anna. "Do you think they'll stay?" she asked, stroking Imp as he playfully tried to nibble her finger. "We could take care of them."

"I don't think they can stay forever," Anna said. "It's too dangerous."

"But where could they go? The diary doesn't say where they really come from."

"Yes it does—one hundred miles east of Assateague."

"That's not a real place, is it?"

Anna looked at her friend in surprise. "You never read *Misty of Chincoteague*?"

Sam shook her head.

"It's about a pony that comes from the island of Assateague, where wild ponies roam. It goes to live with two children on the next island over, called Chincoteague. My dad says . . ." Anna paused for a moment and then hurried on. "He says we'll go there sometime—the islands are down near Virginia somewhere." She leaned forward. "Wild ponies really do live on Assateague. No one knows how they got there, but they've been living on the island for ages and ages. Every year people from Chincoteague go and round up some of them." Anna glanced at the old handwriting again. "Pegasuteague," she said softly. "Pegasus was a flying horse, so Pegasuteague must be the island of the flying horses!"

Sam picked up a piece of paper from the box and unfolded it. It was the one that looked like a treasure map.

"That's Dad's handwriting," said Anna, looking over Sam's shoulder.

"Pegasuteague with a question mark," said Sam, reading from the map. "He made a circle in the ocean. Is this where he thought it might be?" she asked, pointing to the pencil marks.

Anna frowned and bit her lip.

Sam looked back at the map and ran her finger along the dotted line in the ocean from Portsmouth, New Hampshire, down the coast to the emptiness circled in red. "See? Your parents must have been looking for the horses."

Anna nodded dumbly, unable to speak. Yes, it was a sea route. And it was in her father's writing. *"Your parents were lost at sea,"* she heard in her head.

Sam looked at Anna closely. "Why do you tell people your parents are just on vacation?" she asked gently. "You know that's not true, don't you?"

Anna's throat felt like it was closing. She could scarcely breathe. As she stared at the map and the dotted line, she could almost see the doomed boat making its way down the coast, meeting up with the storm, capsizing . . .

She shuddered. The sound of waves crashed in her ears.

ZYXWVUTSRQPONMLKJIHGFEDCBA

The rain had stopped but the clouds were still thick, blanketing the moon. For some reason the streetlight at the corner of Cross Street was out, making the night pitch black. Anna lay in bed, but she wasn't sleeping. Every time she closed her eyes she saw towering waves and a broken mast, swirling waters and then . . . No, she couldn't bear it—she wouldn't allow herself to think or imagine. It wasn't true, it didn't happen.

She sat up. She took deep breaths. "ZYXW-VUTSRQPONMLKJIHGFEDCBA," she whispered fiercely. "ZYXWVUT . . ."

But the little boat tilted in the waves of her imagination. It tilted and then it was over on its side, and her parents were falling into the black sea, the cold waves swallowing them up.

She knew her parents hadn't suddenly changed their plans and gone on a car trip. They had gone sailing. And they weren't lost somewhere, they weren't wandering around in the desert, they weren't about to come home. No. They were never coming home. They were dead. Lost at sea. *Drowned*. She would never see their faces again.

She tried to hold it back, but a wail from deep inside flooded out. She struggled for breath. Now she herself was drowning, drowning in sadness. And then she cried. She cried and she cried. Hot tears burned her face and soaked her pillow.

It was only after her cries had turned to whimpers that she felt a soft warmness brush her ear. She lifted her head, and there, hovering just over her pillow, was H-Rose.

His eyes looked worried as he gazed at Anna. He nuzzled her. And then she slept.

FORTUNES, FORECASTS, AND WARNINGS

Morning. Anna opened her eyes. H-Rose, sound asleep on her pillow, stirred and woke up, too. For several minutes Anna didn't move. Was she going to cry again? She waited, wondering how she felt.

No. She was not going to cry. She did not feel like crying. And although a strange black emptiness sat like a stone inside her, she felt like getting up and figuring things out.

She had slept late, and now hurried to get ready for school. She combed her hair and brushed her teeth and looked in the mirror. She looked just fine.

The horses seemed happy to see Anna when she stepped out the window. They flew down to her immediately and hovered over her. H-Rose had hopped onto her shoulder when she got up, and he was still there, trying hard to keep his balance as she bent over to refill the water bowl.

She lifted H-Rose down gently and said, "You can't come with me to school!" Her eye fell on the diary and she picked it up, flipping through the ancient pages.

Then she noticed something she hadn't seen before—a small, yellowed piece of paper pasted inside the back cover. There was faint writing on it, the same writing as in the rest of the diary:

Song of the Nutberry

Dainty bites, little sizes
Tiny fruit hides surprises
Strange to tell, it always is
Reversed by that which rises.

Anna felt a chill creep up her back. What did it mean? Whatever it was, she felt as if she were reading a card with a fortune on it—and the fortune was hers.

"You okay?" Sam asked Anna, looking at her closely. They were sitting in the cafeteria, eating grilled cheese sandwiches.

Anna sighed. "Yeah," she said. "I'm fine." She lowered her voice. "I found something this morning."

"You did?"

"Listen and tell me what you think this means. I found it at the back of the diary and wrote it down." She pulled a piece of paper out of her pocket and read:

Dainty bites, little sizes
Tiny fruit hides surprises
Strange to tell, it always is
Reversed by that which rises.

Sam frowned. "Tiny fruit?"

"It's called the *Song of the Nutberry*," Anna said meaningfully.

"Ahh. That's interesting. 'Reversed by that which rises.' " Sam thought for a minute. "The nutberry makes you small, and something reverses that. Right?"

"But what?"

"Something that rises." Sam played with the crusts from her sandwich. "The sun rises," she said finally.

"Temperatures rise," offered Anna.

Sam gazed at her sandwich. "You know what?" she said suddenly, looking up.

But Anna had just realized what it was, too. After all, she had made bread with her mother many times and knew what you added to make it rise. "Yeast!" they both shouted together.

Walker was sitting at another table with five or six students. They all looked over at the two girls.

"I was just standing there eating cheese and bread," Sam and Anna said at once. They looked at each other. Then they burst out laughing.

Walker raised his voice. "Hey, what's so funny?" But Anna and Sam were laughing so hard they didn't hear him.

They would not be laughing again that day.

"Don't look now, but Walker's uncle is here," Sam said as she and Anna left school at the end of class.

Anna glanced sideways in the direction Sam was looking. The Ringmaster was leaning against a telephone pole, smoking. He was looking straight at her. He pushed himself away from the pole and started toward them. "He's coming this way," Anna muttered.

"Girlie, I think you and I need to have a little

talk." He pronounced it "LITtle," and Anna could see a fleck of spit fly out of his mouth as he said it.

Sam grabbed Anna's arm and kept walking.

"Hold on there, girlie. What's your hurry?" The Ringmaster's voice was hard. "We got some unsettled business to take care of, don't we?"

"Don't say a word," Anna said in a low voice. "Just keep walking."

The Ringmaster's voice came from behind them now. "My sources suggest you may know something I don't know," he called. "One of these days I just might pay you a visit—with my butterfly net."

The girls hurried on, leaving the Ringmaster staring at their backs. When they arrived at Anna's house, Sam looked at her watch. "I'll meet you in the tree in an hour," she said. "My mother's calling at four." She paused. "She might not remember, but I want to be there just in case . . ."

"Okay," said Anna distractedly. "Meet you in the tree."

Sam turned to go, then turned back and said, "Are you all right? You seem . . ."

"I'm fine," Anna said hurriedly. "It's just that, well, we know everything we need to know now. Except, *how much time do we have left?*"

————

"Not until next week?" Aunt Formaldy's angry voice reached Anna as she opened the back door. "That is not acceptable. A solid week of storms is forecast, beginning tomorrow night, and I want that tree cut down before then!" Anna stood at the door, frozen with horror. "Well, I know it's a fine old tree," her aunt continued peevishly. "But sometimes you just have to act before it's too late. What if a storm blows it onto my house?" She gave an exasperated sigh. "You people seem to put more stock in that tree than in this valuable house and the irreplaceable antiques in it—not to mention my own safety! . . . Very well, then. Next week, if that's the best you can do . . . Yes. Tuesday at nine sharp . . . I'll expect you then." She hung up the phone.

Anna continued to stand in the doorway, half in the house, half out. Now she knew the answer to her question—*there was no time left at all.*

In the distance, the village clock chimed four times. To Anna, it sounded like a warning. She walked slowly to the staircase, her aunt's dreadful words still ringing in her ears. The antique mirror caught her reflection, and she paused to gaze curiously into the blue eyes that looked out at her.

"Sometimes you just have to act before it's too late," her aunt had said.

What about the Humane Society? Anna thought in desperation. They were kind to animals. They would do the right thing. She shook her head. They would take care of the horses—oh, yes. They would take very good care of them, feeding them nutberries, giving them water, putting them in birdcages so they wouldn't fly away and hurt themselves. And the Ringmaster . . .

No, there was no other choice. She had made up her mind.

"Sorry I took so long," Sam said, sitting down on the rocking chair in Anna's tree. Anna was on the yellow sofa, stroking H-Rose's back as if he were a tiny kitten.

"I was waiting for my mom to call," Sam explained. "She didn't, but her secretary did. They're coming this weekend." She looked at the horses fluttering nearby. "It's funny, but I almost wish they weren't. Coming this weekend, I mean." She held out her hand to Imp, who flopped down onto her open palm. "I'd rather be here with these little guys."

Anna nodded. Then she looked away.

Sam studied her friend closely. "What's up?"

Anna glanced down at the table in front of the sofa. "I want to try an experiment."

Sam looked at the plate on the table. There was a piece of bread on it, and a nutberry.

"Experiment . . ." repeated Sam. "How come?"

"My aunt's cutting the tree down next week," Anna said grimly.

Sam gasped. "She can't!"

"She will. She's probably mad because a picture of her in her *authentic* house wasn't in the newspaper but a picture of the tree was. She's afraid it might fall on the house, so she's cutting it down." Anna bit her lip. "It's the only place the horses are safe. I have to save them."

A look of alarm flashed in Sam's eyes. "How?" She looked as if she did not want to hear the answer.

Anna took a deep breath. "I'm taking the horses to Pegasuteague," she blurted out.

The color drained from Sam's face. "You can't!" she cried. "You can't, you can't, you can't!"

Anna reached out her hand and let it fall to her side. "I have to." She hurried on, trying to explain things to herself as well as to Sam. "Don't you see, Sam? If I don't take them, they'll die. They can't live without nutberries!" She looked up at Cyclone, who had been hovering nearby all afternoon. "I think they're waiting for someone to rescue them, to help them find their way back. And I'm the only one who can."

A sudden forlorn expression crossed Sam's face,

but it disappeared quickly. "You don't know how to get there either, Anna," she pointed out.

"Sure I do," said Anna, trying to sound confident. "I'll just follow the map—head straight east until I get to the o-ocean." She stumbled over that word. "And then just turn south and follow the coast until I get to Assateague."

"And then . . ."

"And then straight out to . . . straight out to sea," said Anna.

"And then . . ." Sam continued, a worried expression on her face. "Are you planning on coming back anytime?"

"Of course I am." Anna looked earnestly at her friend. "That's what the experiment is for. To see if I can really change sizes the way we think." She leaned forward. "Look," she said, "it will be fine. All I have to do is get the horses to Pegasuteague safe and sound. Then I can fly back to shore—maybe to Chincoteague—and send Cyclone back to Pegasuteague." She flipped a hand. "See? Easy!"

"Easy. Huh," said Sam. "Then what?"

"Well, then I'll eat some bread, get back to my normal size, and . . . and . . . call the police or somebody. I can say I ran away from home and want to go back." She smiled. "It's simple."

Sam nodded reluctantly. "I guess it could work. If

you make it that far." She stood up and paced back and forth. "I'm coming with you."

"You know you can't, Sam. I won't be missed. But you will. There are people who care about you."

A look of surprise flashed across Sam's face. "Yes," she said. "I guess so. But how can you say *you* won't be missed?" She paused. Then she said, "*I'll miss you, Anna.*"

Anna gave her friend a grateful smile. "I have to see if this works first," she said, and then, before she lost her courage, she reached over and popped the nutberry into her mouth, tasting the sweet lemony center before swallowing it.

Nothing happened.

Then, just as Anna was wondering if they had been wrong about nutberries, she was suddenly plunging down into space, falling and falling. The loud whining noise was deafening, and she held her hands to her ears as she felt herself shrinking. And then there was silence. And darkness.

"Can you help me out of here?" Anna yelled. "I'm stuck in my pants leg."

"You . . . imploded," said Sam, lifting the clothes gently off Anna.

Anna looked up at her, trying not to panic. She did not like being small, not one bit. "Can you give me a piece of bread? Quick?"

Sam tore off a tiny piece and bent down and handed it to Anna. She looked as scared as Anna felt.

Anna popped the bread into her mouth and swallowed, hardly taking the time to chew it. Sam had moved back to the other end of the branch, as if she thought she might be hit by exploding parts. "Well?" she said.

"I don't feel anything ye—" Anna suddenly gasped and held on to her stomach. *Bam bam bam!* She felt as if she were a balloon being blown up. All of a sudden there she was, back to normal.

Sam handed her her clothes and said anxiously, "Are you okay? It looks . . . painful."

Anna felt a little out of breath. "It doesn't hurt," she assured Sam. "It's a weird feeling, but it doesn't hurt at all."

Neither said anything for a few minutes. Anna finished dressing and sat back down on the sofa. The horses peered at the girls from the branches overhead as if they were waiting for something. Anna took a few deep breaths, trying to calm herself, as Sam paced back and forth distractedly.

"We have five days before your aunt cuts down the tree," Sam said. "We'll think of something before then . . ." She stopped.

Anna was shaking her head. "We don't have five

days. We don't even have a day," she said, trying to keep her voice from trembling. "Starting tomorrow, there's a week of storms coming, and it will be too dangerous to fly. And after that . . ." Her voice broke. She could not bear thinking about her tree.

"Are you saying . . .?"

Anna nodded. "Tonight," she said grimly.

Sam looked stricken.

"I'll need some things," Anna said, trying to comfort her friend. "Can you get them for me?"

LATE AND DARK

Anna looked at the clock on the little table next to the yellow sofa. Seven o'clock. And it was already dark. Soon she would be flying to the coast and then out over the ocean. She imagined the waves grabbing her and dragging her down. "I don't want to go!" she heard a small voice inside her cry. "I'm too afraid!" She stood up and began pacing. There was no way she was going to be able to follow through on this plan. It was crazy. Reckless. Stupid. Anyone could see that. She couldn't be expected to do this. No one would blame her if she didn't.

What had she been thinking? It would be smarter—*better*—to stay here safe and sound. She breathed a sigh of relief. She did not have to go, after all! The horses would be fine. Even in cages. Why should she have to risk her life for them?

H-Rose, balancing unsteadily on her shoulder, suddenly nuzzled her cheek. His soft nose was warm, and she could feel his breath. Red Sox and Yankee, Sunbeam and Moonbeam, Violet and Fugitive and Imp and Beauty, all fluttered about nearby, as if they were waiting for her. And Cyclone gazed steadily at Anna from an overhanging branch, his big brown eyes full of trust. Anna sat down on the sofa and rocked back and forth, her arms wrapped tightly around herself.

Sam, carrying a small bag, stepped through the window. "Are you all right?" she asked in alarm when she saw Anna scrunched over.

"I'm fine," Anna said, sitting up quickly. H-Rose slipped off her shoulder and fluttered onto her lap. "I'm just thinking about the trip."

Sam studied her anxiously. "You're sure you want to go?"

"It's not that I *want* to." Anna grimaced. "I have to."

Sam looked at her friend with respect. She dumped her bag onto the sofa, and out tumbled a collection of Suzy camping equipment and hiking clothes. There was a warm jacket. And some mittens and a hat. And pants and shirts and shoes and sneakers. There was a purple backpack with a wee water bottle in the side pocket. Anna noticed that it was already filled.

The jacket was black, with fake fur trim around the hood and the cuffs. Anna picked up the pack and unzipped the little zipper. Inside were several bits of bread, each one wrapped carefully in plastic, and a tiny bag filled with nutberries. The outside pockets of the pack were stuffed with extra nutberries.

"You're the best," Anna said.

Sam shook her head doubtfully. "If I were, I wouldn't be letting you do this." She paused. "Or I would be coming with you. Or . . . I don't know," she finished lamely.

Anna smiled. "You would be doing just what you're doing—being my best friend."

Two little round spots of red appeared on Sam's cheeks. "Same here," she said.

The two girls didn't say anything for a bit. Then Anna sighed and stood up. "It should be late enough now, don't you think?" Her stomach felt queasy, and she wondered if she would be able to swallow anything. She picked up a nutberry and checked to make sure her Suzy clothes and backpack were nearby.

Sam nodded. "Okay."

"Here goes," said Anna, and she quickly popped the nutberry into her mouth. She swallowed, and soon the familiar swooshing and whining filled her ears. A moment later she was putting on the Suzy clothes and slinging the backpack onto her back. She looked up at Sam, whose pale face seemed even paler now, and said, "I think I'm getting used to this!"

Sam bit her lip nervously. "I'll check and make sure the coast is clear."

"Cyclone!" called Anna in her small voice. In an instant the stallion, who now seemed very large indeed, swooped down to stand patiently while she jumped onto his back. Together they hurried up to the lookout, where Sam was peering through the leaves.

"There's no one around," Sam whispered. "And the moon is bright and there are lots of stars." Her voice trembled a little as she spoke.

The horses had followed them to the top of the tree. They seemed to sense that something was about to happen.

Anna took a deep breath. "I guess I'd better get going, then." She looked at Sam gratefully. "Thanks for being such a good friend."

Suddenly Cyclone let out a sharp cry. The horses reared up as the faint odor of cigarette smoke floated into the night air.

"The Ringmaster!" gasped Sam. Cyclone stood

like a statue, his ears twitching, as if he were listening to the sound of footsteps echoing on the empty street.

"All right, girlie, I know you're up there." The voice was low and flat and final.

For five seconds the girls stared at each other in horror.

Then, finally, Anna said, "I'll see you soon, Sam!" She bent over to whisper in Cyclone's ear. "Let's get out of here. Come on, Cyclone, I'm taking you home!"

Instantly Cyclone, with Anna holding on tight, flew up out of the tree. He whinnied. Anna turned and saw that the other horses were right behind them as they swooped up into the night sky. Sunbeam's golden mane flashed in the moonlight, and Imp was speeding past Fugitive as if this were a race. But where was H-Rose?

Suddenly a small high-pitched cry pierced the night. Cyclone wheeled and turned. Something terrible must have happened. Below, Anna could see the horses flying in confused circles, parting and coming together again, then spinning out in different directions. She looked down.

And there, standing in the middle of her street, was the Ringmaster. He held a long-poled butterfly net. And something was thrashing about inside it.

H-Rose.

Before Anna could think what to do, Cyclone swooped straight for the street and the Ringmaster. Anna could see the man's face in the streetlight now. His mouth curled up into a grimace of triumph, his eyes gleaming with satisfaction.

With a sudden plunge, Cyclone dived at his head. The Ringmaster swatted the air, looking about wildly. Cyclone rose into the air with Anna hanging on, then once again dive-bombed the Ringmaster, this time knocking the cigarette out of his mouth. With a snarl the man spun around. His right hand held on to the butterfly net with H-Rose flapping his wings helplessly inside, while his left hand madly batted the air.

And then the Ringmaster saw Anna, holding on to Cyclone's neck, her tiny legs wrapped tight around the stallion's back.

For a long moment he stared at the doll-sized girl, his eyes wide with surprise. Then, without warning, he lunged.

Dropping the butterfly net, he clawed at Cyclone with both hands. As if he were moving in slow motion, Anna watched the Ringmaster's fingers reach for them, so close she could see the dirt under his huge fingernails. "Cyclone!" Anna cried as she felt a powerful blow strike the side of the stallion and a giant finger begin to close around her leg.

He had them, he had them both.

The stallion shrieked, and all at once the horses rushed at the Ringmaster's face. Their tiny hooves struck at his eyes, their teeth nipped his nose and cheeks. The Ringmaster grunted and gasped, but he would not let go of Anna and her horse.

And then Anna saw a figure shoot out of the shadows like a cannonball, right into the Ringmaster's legs. It was Sam. With an angry cry the Ringmaster toppled over, releasing his hold. Grabbing the net, Sam freed the struggling colt. H-Rose bolted out of the Ringmaster's reach.

Cyclone shot into the sky. H-Rose and the rest of the horses followed. They were safe.

Anna looked down. She could see the Ringmaster below them. He had picked himself up from the ground and was looking up at them, his face filled with rage. Sam was nowhere to be seen. As Anna watched, the Ringmaster bent down and picked up three nutberries that had fallen from Anna's pack. He examined them carefully. Then he put them in his pocket.

"I get it. I know your secret, girlie!" he yelled up at her. "I know your secret!"

PART 3

WE'RE FLYING!

With the moon at their back, Anna urged Cyclone on toward the coast, the image of the Ringmaster's fury still burning in her eyes. *He knows. He knows the secret of the nutberry.*

They were traveling at high speed now, and the world below sped by in a flash.

There's no turning back, thought Anna.

Her house, cold and ugly with Aunt Formaldy and her horrible antiques, suddenly seemed warm and safe to her. Her books, her tree, Sam—how beautiful they all were. The wind was cold on Anna's nose, and she buried her face in Cyclone's mane. Doubts crowded into her head: she was just eleven years old, she was crazy to have attempted this, she didn't know anything about flying or navigating or anything. And worst of all, the angry ocean was ahead.

ZYXWVUT . . .

"Stop that!" Anna scolded herself.

Cyclone pulled up sharply to a slower speed, and the rest of the horses slowed down with him. He whinnied softly. It seemed as if he were asking her a question.

"No, not you, I was talking to me," Anna said, patting Cyclone on the neck a little sheepishly. "It's okay. I'm sorry, everything is fine."

Cyclone snorted and shook his head and once again raced at full speed into the night.

Widely scattered lights whizzed by below—street-lights, house lights, porch lights, headlights. People were asleep or going about mysterious late-night business, all of them unaware that far above them a flock of tiny horses and a small girl were heading east, toward the sea.

They had not been flying for long when Anna spotted a thick clump of lights shining against a great blackness. It was the seaport of Portsmouth, asleep and silent. Nothing moved but an occasional headlight. Beyond the town lay the black nothing-ness of the Atlantic Ocean.

Anna breathed in sharply. The air here was damp and smelled of seaweed and fish. Far below, Anna could see the tide rolling out. This was where her parents had begun their voyage: Portsmouth. "New Hampshire's jewel" her father had called it.

"Easy now, slow down," Anna urged. But it wasn't necessary. Cyclone was already slowing and wheeling, circling gently down toward the white beach, smelling the familiar smell of sea and sand. The tiny horses flew low over the gently sloping shore, and Anna could see the waves breaking white in the moonlight.

It was warmer down here, ten or fifteen feet above the shore. And it was quiet. Anna could see a sandal lying above the tideline, left there by some beachgoer during the summer, maybe. Its size was a shock, for Anna had almost forgotten that she and the horses were small, smaller even than the seagulls one could usually find on the beach. At the thought of gulls, Anna looked around her nervously. *Do they attack creatures like us?* she wondered.

The tide was going out, and the beach looked vast and lonely. A crab, bigger than Anna, scuttled down to the water. "I don't like being here," she said out loud. But the horses swooped over the sand and raced along the shore, their wings almost touching the water. They climbed and dived and grazed their feet on the tops of little waves. H-Rose stopped long enough to poke his nose at a starfish, then shot up

into the sky, letting himself glide back down, his
wings barely moving.

Cyclone did not play, however. He seemed to
watch the others indulgently for a while, then he
whinnied, as if asking, "What next?"

Anna had memorized the map, how the coast
curved inward where the islands were. She could see
it all clearly in her head. Tugging gently on the stallion's mane, she leaned to the right, southward, and
whispered, "Let's go to Pegasuteague!" He seemed
to understand which way she wanted him to go.
With a mighty movement of his wings, he sped
across the sky like a shooting star. The rest of the
tiny horses followed close behind.

They were headed south. Except for the occasional snorting of the other horses, the silence was
complete.

The moon was high now, and stars in great num-
bers dotted the black sky. Living in New Hampshire,
Anna was used to seeing stars, but never had she
seen anything like this. The Milky Way stretched
above her, a wide highway of white.

She wondered if astronauts felt like this—calm
and awestruck at the same time, as if their problems
had shrunk to the size of grains of sand. Aunt
Formaldy—how small she was. Laughable, even.

Walker—how ridiculous! Greeley, New Hampshire, quaint and pretty and cold and remote. Anna's loneliness and anger, even her sadness, seemed smaller up here. Up here she felt hope. Only the thought of the black sea far below could frighten her.

Anna looked down. Another glowing jewel lay below her now, a galaxy of lights. Was she flying upside down and seeing the Milky Way? She leaned over to get a better view. A thousand skyscrapers pierced the night sky, all of them lighted from top to bottom. In the middle, a colossal pointed spire rose above the rest, and Anna realized it was the Empire State Building. She was flying over New York City.

She could see little lights moving—cars and trucks and buses, even at this late hour. As she watched, some of the lights detached themselves from the earth and began to rise upward, over the skyscrapers, up and up . . .

The word "airplane" had just begun to form in Anna's mind when all of a sudden a scream shattered the night's silence like a sledgehammer, as if an angry god had let out a world-ending roar. A huge silver shape tore out of the blackness, lights flashing on its wingtips and gleaming in its windows. It was a jet, a jumbo jet, and it was right there in front of them. It was so big and fast and loud that for a minute Anna could not make sense of what she was seeing.

A face in the cockpit stared out at her in shocked disbelief, eyes popping, mouth a large O. And then it was gone, leaving behind a gust of wind that bowled them right over. Anna held on tight, and in a moment it was calm again.

She looked around. They were all still together, the stallion and the mares and the fillies and the colts and H-Rose, and they were soaring now, wings stretched out, sailing along as if nothing had happened.

An hour went by, or maybe a year; Anna couldn't tell. It was as if she were in a different dimension, a place that was warm and cold, safe and dangerous, happy and sad all at the same time. Where did Anna end and Cyclone begin? She didn't know anymore. But she felt alive. She felt free.

She leaned over and patted Cyclone's neck, feeling strong and powerful inside.

"Wheeeee!" she cried. "We're flying!"

SURROUNDED
BY DEEP SEA

They flew on and on, following the coast. The air became warmer and wetter. Anna pulled off her ski hat. She unzipped her jacket. Puffs of fog appeared and disappeared, and a warm breeze blew in her face. It was still dark when she took her jacket off and tied it around her waist.

At last a faint glow warmed up the east, and Anna could see the outline of the coast become clearer and clearer. It was early dawn, scarcely morning, when she saw the island of Assateague.

It was easy to recognize. Long and thin, it was like no other island. Tucked in close to Assateague was the island of Chincoteague, and Anna could see the lights of houses, warm and inviting. For a moment she longed to be there, safe.

But one hundred miles farther out in the fog, if

the diary was right, lay the undiscovered island of the flying horses, Pegasuteague. In spite of the warm sea breeze, Anna felt a chill come over her.

One hundred miles, with nothing below but the hungry sea.

Cyclone whinnied suddenly and swooped down low over Assateague. The faint rays of dawn were barely enough to see by, but Anna could smell the sea and hear the thundering waves . . . But no, that wasn't waves she heard, it was horses. She peered down at them, a group of about twelve. They looked very much like her own horses—without wings, though, and of course much, much bigger. They ran across the saltmarsh and stopped to munch the sea grass on the dunes.

Anna was seeing Assateague at last.

Suddenly Cyclone seemed to sense that he was near home. He raised his head, his ears twitching back and forth, his nose in the air. He whinnied loudly and swooped down over the island, flying back and forth as if to get his bearings. The others followed closely behind.

Then, without warning, he veered out over the ocean. Immediately it felt colder and windier. Anna peered down. No trees or sand or comforting lights. Just the gray sea, the low sun reflecting off the sharp peaks of the waves. She closed her eyes.

They had left the coast behind.

Anna had a clear picture of her father's hand-drawn map in her head—the red circle around nothing, the word "Pegasuteague?" written in her father's handwriting. Straight out in the ocean, that's where it was, a hundred miles or more away from land, lonely, isolated, and completely surrounded by cold, deep sea.

The lights of the coast disappeared almost immediately, and darkness spread out below like a black monster waiting. What if they couldn't find the island? What if it didn't exist at all? What if there was nothing out here but emptiness and cold water?

With an effort, Anna opened her eyes and tried to see ahead. A dim yellowness shrouded everything. "It must be the sun beginning to shine on the fog," she said to herself. She urged the stallion on and hugged him with her arms. She could feel his warmth right through her clothes.

And his sweat.

He was getting tired. She looked back over her shoulder at the rest of the horses. Was it her imagination, or were their wings moving more slowly?

They must be worn out, Anna thought. Of course. They were completely exhausted. They were probably thirsty, too. She had made a terrible mistake, not stopping for water and a rest. *Should we turn back?*

she wondered. But Cyclone flew on, and Anna knew she could not turn him around even if she tried.

The air was heavy, and it pressed down on them. Cyclone's head seemed to sag. Anna hugged him. "You can find it, I know you can," she encouraged him. But something odd was happening. The air seemed to be filling up with moisture. Anna took a deep breath, but she still felt breathless. Cyclone snorted, and Anna could feel them both sink a little.

A tickling sensation started in the pit of her stomach and spread up her spine and into her armpits. It was fear.

Suddenly the feeble light was extinguished, as if a giant had blown it out like a candle. Anna and her horses were pitched into total darkness. She opened her eyes as wide as they would go. There was nothing, nothing to see. Never before had she experienced such blackness, such complete absence of light. Always there had been something—a faintly glimmering star or a distant streetlight or *something*. But now emptiness surrounded her on all sides. She could not tell up from down, right from left.

The air was cold and damp, so thick and misty that she could scarcely catch her breath, and she gasped for air. *Calm, be calm*, she urged herself.

And then she realized what this was. She must be

in the fog of Pegasuteague. It was *supposed* to be like this! It was this fog that had kept the island hidden from view. They must be really close . . .

And just as this thought came to her, they were caught in a spinning vortex, a whirlwind that grabbed them and spun them around and around, downward, downward, faster and faster, plunging them toward the sea and its frigid waves.

"Cyclone!" she screamed in desperation. "Come on!" She could feel Cyclone straining beneath her, but it was no use. The wind whirled about them and they all tumbled over and over, head over heels. Anna tried to scream and held on to the stallion's mane. She thought her fingers would break. The blast of air whistled past her ears and blew her mouth open and kept her scream from escaping from her throat.

Down and down they spiraled. And then a spray of icy saltwater hit her.

This is why the island is unknown, thought Anna dimly. *Anyone who comes near it is killed.*

She thought of her mother and father.

"We have *all* been lost at sea," she heard herself say out loud. And then everything became dark emptiness.

DREAM SONG

The song flitted in and out of her dreams. She was falling, she was running, she was flying, chasing monsters and being chased, and through it all she could hear the sad melody. *"What'll I do-o-o-o . . . when you-ou-ou . . . are far awayyyyyy . . ."*

Anna turned over. She wondered what was wrong with her bed; why was it so uncomfortable? She opened her eyes and found herself staring up into her tree, the pear-shaped leaves trembling slightly in the salty breeze. *How did I get outside?* she wondered. *Why aren't I in my bed?* She sat up. The smell of sea and salt was too strong to ignore now.

This wasn't her tree. This wasn't her home. Where *was* she?

"And I am blue-ue-ue . . . what'll I do?" The haunting song faded in and out through the leftover wisps of her dream, ending in a sob.

Am I awake or asleep? Anna wondered. She stood up and looked around her. She was standing in a grove of giant trees.

Trees exactly like her own tree at home.

A pear-shaped leaf as big as she was had fallen to the ground beside her, and a nutberry the size of an apple lay next to it. Anna shook her head, trying to clear it. What had happened? She looked around.

Behind her was a sandy beach. Gentle waves slid over the sand and settled silently back into an almost invisible sea.

A strange sparkly light glinted off the white sand and the leaves of the trees and the tall grass. It seemed like morning. But something hid the ocean from her. It wasn't darkness exactly. It was more like a glimmery mist.

A movement caught Anna's eye. A group of flying horses rose up out of a nearby tree and wheeled across the treetops. They looked just like her own horses, only she didn't recognize any of them. There were at least twenty. They soared and dived and played in the strange, still morning. Another flock of horses swooped out of a tree, and Anna spotted a tiny colt among them. It was H-Rose. And there was Imp—and Red Sox!

"I am not dreaming," Anna told herself. "We made it!" She looked about eagerly for the other horses, and there, just beyond the shade of the huge tree she stood under, was Cyclone. He was standing as still as a statue. Only his great wings, spread out behind him, fluttered almost imperceptibly. He was gazing at her. What was that look in his eyes?

But fragments of her dream still drifted about in her head. She could still hear that song rising and falling in her ears. Her mother's voice, the old words, the aching memory. She wondered if she had hit her head. She shook it violently. There. It was gone. All she could hear now was the sound of the waves lapping the shore gently, the leaves rustling softly in the trees, and the horses whinnying back and forth to each other.

Anna realized she was very thirsty. Was there water here? she wondered. She watched a cloud of horses settle down in the distance, beyond the farthest trees. Maybe that's where the water is, she thought.

The cool morning air smelled sweet, and Anna walked through it feeling very odd, as if she were watching herself from ten feet away. She could see herself, eight inches high, the only human being on this strange island, stepping over pebbles as if they were rocks, jumping over twigs, standing waist-high in grass. Small as a mouse.

Anna looked up at the sky with alarm. Were there hawks about? Owls? Was she, could she be . . . prey? Suddenly she felt weak and vulnerable.

But the beach was silent and empty, and the sky was filled only with horses. She breathed a sigh of relief.

There's nothing and nobody here but me and the horses, she thought.

And then there it was again, the singing. *"With only dreams of yo-ou . . ."* Anna walked slowly toward the voice.

It was not a dream.

TIME STANDS STILL

Anna saw her bending over a scallop shell, her long red hair tied behind her. Water dripped from her hands, and Anna could see that she was washing her face.

"Momm . . . Mommy?" said Anna. "Is that you?"

The woman with the red hair looked up. She rubbed her eyes and blinked hard and stared.

"Anna?" she whispered.

And then time stood still, the earth stopped moving on its axis, the waves were halted halfway to shore. And in that frozen moment, in that space between seeing and understanding, Anna and her mother stared at each other until at last they understood.

Anna's happy sobs and her mother's cries of joy

filled the island. They hugged and they laughed and they cried. The horses stopped flitting about from tree to tree and hurried to see what the commotion was about.

"What is happening?" cried a frightened voice from above. Anna looked up. It was her father, mounted on the back of a black stallion, rushing to the scene, an expression of terror on his face. He dismounted almost before the horse touched the ground and ran to his wife.

And then he saw Anna.

"Daddy!" Anna cried.

Her father stood for half a moment, staring in disbelief at his daughter. Then he ran and scooped her up in his arms. "Anna? My own dear Anna?"

This scene went on for such a long time that the horses began to snort and stamp and whinny nervously. Cyclone swooped over to stand protectively beside Anna, eyeing her parents suspiciously.

But Anna's smile, which spread from one ear to the other, was enough to convince even Cyclone that she was absolutely fine.

STORIES

Anna was sitting in her father's lap, just as she had when she was a little girl. Her mother was holding her hand, gazing at her and saying over and over again, "I cannot believe it." And H-Rose, who had tried to squeeze in between Anna and her mother, had finally fallen asleep at Anna's feet.

Anna and her parents had been holding one another for two hours, and until now they had been too overwhelmed to say much more than "I am so happy" and "Are you fine, really?" and "I can't believe it."

But finally they were able to speak about other things, and Anna heard her parents' story.

They had been looking for the horses, just as Anna and Sam had thought. "We expected it to be an adventure," Anna's mother explained. "We didn't really believe the horses could exist. Well, we did a little."

The trip had gone smoothly until, not long after they had passed Assateague and headed out to sea, a violent storm had capsized their sailboat. "We feared we would go down with the ship," said Anna's mother. "All we could think of was you." To their surprise, they had awakened on this fog-shrouded island. Here they saw the very winged horses they had been searching for.

But their excitement was soon drowned by horror. They were trapped. There was nothing left of their boat but planks and debris. They decided to try to make a raft and float back to the coast. But hunger was their first concern, and they were dismayed to find that nothing seemed to thrive on the island but the winged horses and the trees. It did not take long for them to realize that the sole source of nutrition for the horses was the nutberries, and with great uneasiness they finally decided to try some. Of course they shrank. There was nothing they could do then but make their home with the horses.

Anna told her mother and father about Hurricane Bela and about how much she loved the horses and how worried she had been. She told them about Sam.

And she told them about Aunt Formaldy.

"Oh, my dear little Anna," her father said, shaking his head sadly. "I can only imagine how it must have been for you."

But Aunt Formaldy did not matter to Anna anymore. Aunt Formaldy no longer had any power over her.

"You'll like Sam," said Anna, her eyes sparkling. "As soon as we're home—" But the look on her parents' faces stopped her. Their faces were sad, almost horrified.

"Oh, Anna," her mother said quickly, "I am sure she is just wonderful, and I wish we could meet her. But . . ." Her voice trailed off and she looked helplessly at her husband.

Anna's father was grave. "Anna, my dear little palindrome, there is no way home. We are stuck here forever, small and helpless."

"But you don't understand!" cried Anna. "We can fly on the horses to Chincoteague! And when we're there we can rent a car and drive home, or take a bus, or an airplane, or . . . or walk! It doesn't matter!" She laughed happily, looking from her mother to her father and back again. But their eyes remained solemn, and they smiled with effort.

"You forget, Anna," said her father gently. "You

forget—we're very . . . we're quite . . . small. Life back home would be . . . impossible." He held out his hands to her. "But we have each other, and that's what's important."

But Anna knew something they did not know, and now she told them about the bread and yeast and the amazing powers it had to counteract the effect of the nutberries. She recited the *Song of the Nutberry* for them and described the strange sensation of growing suddenly large.

At first her parents did not dare to believe her. However, at last they began to hope that what Anna was saying was true. After all, so many strange and wonderful things had happened, why not one more?

They stood on the beach in the darkness just before dawn. A soft breeze whistled mournfully through the beach grass, and invisible waves lapped the shore. The moon, though shrouded by the mists of Pegasuteague, filtered through enough to cast a pale light over the sand. Anna could see her own tiny horses stamping their feet anxiously nearby. "They know we're leaving," she whispered to her parents.

H-Rose fluttered over to Anna and nudged her with his nose. Anna felt a rush of tenderness sweep over her. "You take care of yourself, little one," she mumbled, throwing her arms around him. "And no more wandering around in hurricanes!" He was so little she could almost have picked him up in her own small arms. She touched his side and could feel the little ridge of scar under his white coat.

Cyclone, who had been stamping his feet and shaking his head, gave a small whinny. Anna's parents were already mounted on their horses. Now Anna pulled herself onto the stallion's back and said, "I'm ready."

They rose up into the sky, and Anna took one last look behind her. Each of the tiny horses watched her—H-Rose and Beauty, Red Sox and Yankee, Sunbeam and Moonbeam, Violet and Fugitive and Imp. "Goodbye!" she shouted, knowing it was unlikely she would ever see any of them again. "Goodbye!"

A LAST
GOODBYE

It was the perfect place, right on the beach at Chincoteague, a lonely cottage with a white picket fence around a tidy little yard. A maple tree stood bright red in a corner of the yard, illuminated by a porch light. Underneath the tree was a bench, and on the bench were gardening shears and a pair of gloves. Chrysanthemums bloomed in the garden.

A mother and a father must live here, and their children, at least two. Anna could tell because of their clothes, which had dried in the evening breeze and still hung on the clothesline that stretched from the porch to the maple tree. Four pairs of shoes were lined up neatly on the porch.

"Just what we need!" Anna exclaimed happily.

"Made to order," Mr. Farrington agreed, looking up at the pants and shirts. "We can mail them back later."

Mrs. Farrington shook her head in wonder. "It's hard to imagine wearing those giant clothes!"

The three of them stood quietly for a moment, the fresh-mown grass tickling their knees, the pre-dawn dew cool on their faces. "I guess I'm ready," said Anna. And then she looked at Cyclone.

The stallion's brown eyes flickered. *He knows this is goodbye forever.* Suddenly Anna's throat ached, as if something were squeezing it. Cyclone lowered his head to hers and pressed his warm nose against her hair, making a soft whickering sound.

"I will never, ever forget you, I promise," Anna finally managed to whisper, looking into his eyes. He gazed back at her questioningly. *He is telling me to stay.*

"I can't," she murmured. "I'm going home." Cyclone's nostrils quivered, and he nudged Anna's cheek gently. She threw her arms around him and buried her face in his mane, choking back tears. "I'm going to miss you so much."

Finally Anna turned to her parents, who stood quietly in the grass. They were holding hands and watching her, their eyes solemn but full of hope. "Shall we have a bite of bread?" asked her father gently.

Anna nodded, then turned back to the white stallion. "I'll be back someday," she whispered suddenly. "I will."

FULL TO BURSTING

It was almost dark when the Farringtons arrived in Greeley. Mr. Farrington peered out of the car window as he brought the rented car to a stop in front of the old Farrington house. "Home at last!"

Anna's heart was pounding with joy, and she jumped out of the car and ran up to the front door. She rang the doorbell and then knocked loudly.

After a moment or two Aunt Formaldy opened the door. She looked down at Anna. "Good heavens. Who are you?"

Anna smiled. "Hello, Aunt Formaldy."

Her aunt scowled. "What, may I ask, are you doing at my front door? I believe I have informed you that if you must enter my house, you will do so through the *back* door."

"Hello, Formy," said Anna's father, his voice coming suddenly out of the darkness behind Anna.

"I think you're mistaken. Anna can come in any door she feels like."

Aunt Formaldy took a step backward and gawked at the Farringtons, her face turning as white as the pearl necklace around her neck. "Arthur. Jane." She stood frozen inside the door, apparently unable to speak. At last she said, "Well! Well! What a . . . what a pleasant surprise! I thought your boat was lost at sea!"

"It was," Mr. Farrington said, stepping into the house with Anna's mother and closing the door behind them. "But we weren't." He looked around. "What odd things you have done to our home. I hardly know where I am."

He looked at Anna. "You poor dear girl. How awful it must have been for you."

Anna, full to bursting with joy, could hardly keep from jumping up and down. "Very, very awful—terrible!" she said happily.

Aunt Formaldy was still standing with her mouth open. Now she smiled grotesquely. "Oh, yes, it has been quite trying without you, Arthur. I can promise you that! Just dreadful! Why, your daughter and I have been completely bereft! Thank goodness we have had each other."

Mrs. Farrington shook her head. "I'm afraid—"

But at that moment the doorbell rang. "I'll get it!" said Anna, so full of happiness she had to do something. She ran to the door and opened it. It was all the members of the Historical Society.

Ms. Axelrod smiled at Anna and said in a conspiratorial voice, "Is your aunt available? We know it's late, but we just couldn't wait to tell her that she has been unanimously voted in as our president." She turned to the other members, who were all beaming and nodding. Mr. Cincinnati, from the *Greeley Times*, was there, too. With his camera.

Anna invited the members and Mr. Cincinnati into the living room, where Aunt Formaldy, who was struggling to recover from her shock, had seated herself stiffly on a chair near the telephone. On seeing the Historical Society, she stood up a little shakily. "Ah, my dears! What a delightful surprise to see you here. I was just thinking today what a dedicated and inspiring group you are."

"We have a little announcement to make," Ms. Axelrod said, looking exceedingly pleased. She gave a formal cough. "Formaldy Farrington, we are deeply honored to offer you the—"

And then they noticed Mr. and Mrs. Farrington. They stared in astonishment. "Arthur and Jane!" cried Mrs. Farnsworth. "Can it really be you?"

Mrs. Farrington smiled happily and replied, "We're so glad to be home at last!"

"How extraordinary!" exclaimed Ms. Axelrod.

"How miraculous!" cried Mrs. Bemis. "This is wonderful!"

After welcoming hugs all around, Ms. Axelrod turned to Aunt Formaldy. "What a wonderful surprise for you! A night full of happy news!"

Aunt Formaldy smiled a steely smile. "Happy news indeed. Simply overwhelmed! Now, you were saying?"

But then the doorbell rang again, and before Anna could answer it, Sam was barreling into the living room, barefoot, wearing purple pajamas, and out of breath. "Anna! You're alive!" she said as she threw her arms around her friend and lifted her right up off her feet. "I've been watching your house every minute! You're back! You're back! You're back!" she cried happily.

"You must be Sam," said Mrs. Farrington, smiling. "Anna has told us so much about you!"

Sam turned and gaped at Mrs. Farrington. "Y-you . . ." she stammered, and then she saw Mr. Farrington, smiling the same wide smile that Anna was smiling, the same smile Sam had seen in the photograph so long ago. "You—"

"I found them!" exclaimed Anna. And then she

stopped and looked at the assembled guests, who seemed slightly bewildered. "I mean, I'll tell you later," she added in a low voice.

Aunt Formaldy coughed delicately. "Ms. Axelrod, you were saying?"

"Well," Ms. Axelrod said, smiling, "with all this happiness tonight, perhaps . . ."

"Yes, yes, great happiness. All of this is a dream come true for . . . uh . . . for . . . my dear niece and me! But . . ."

Mr. Farrington, who had been smiling happily at his daughter and her friend, now turned to Formaldy. "A dream come true for you and . . . who?"

"What? Oh, for my dear niece and me," answered Aunt Formaldy, gesturing impatiently toward Anna.

"And who, may I ask, is the 'dear niece' you refer to?"

Aunt Formaldy frowned with irritation. "Why . . . *her*," she said, pointing at Anna.

"And her name is?" asked Anna's father, looking quizzical.

"Why, it's . . . it's . . . uh . . . Well, I am sure you know your own child's name . . ." Aunt Formaldy's voice trailed off.

There was a shocked silence as the members of

the Historical Society looked at one another in wonder.

"You don't know our daughter's name?" cried Mrs. Farrington, incredulous.

"It just goes to show you," Anna whispered to Sam, and they both laughed so hard they nearly choked.

When their laughter subsided, Ms. Axelrod spoke up. "Perhaps . . . Yes, I think it's best we go home. You must have so much to catch up on." She gave Aunt Formaldy a strange look.

Aunt Formaldy's hand flew to her throat. "No, do stay! We are quite happy to hear whatever it is you would like to announce!" she said as she nervously fiddled with her necklace.

Mr. Farrington stared at his wife's pearls draped around Formaldy Farrington's neck. Then he looked at the expensive antiques. "Of course, Formaldy, we will want to know what has happened to Anna's inheritance. There will have to be a public hearing on the matter."

"A public . . ." Aunt Formaldy's face seemed to crumple. "A puh . . . a puh . . ."

Every member of the Historical Society gasped and turned to Mr. Farrington. "We have been sadly mistaken, I'm afraid," Ms. Axelrod said grimly.

"Sadly mistaken. It seems to me that you have arrived just in the nick of time." She turned to Aunt
Formaldy. "We will say goodbye to you now." And
then the Greeley Historical Society marched out the
door.

The photographer from the *Greeley Times* looked
crestfallen for a moment. Then he brightened and,
perhaps imagining a truly sensational headline,
snapped a photograph of Aunt Formaldy just as she
buried her face in her hands.

"You have exactly one hour," Anna's father announced to his shaken stepsister, "to pack your
things and leave."

And then, as Aunt Formaldy collapsed into one
of her authentic historic chairs, Anna, Sam, and
Mr. and Mrs. Farrington all walked up the stairs,
squeezed through Anna's tiny room, and stepped out
her window into the Justin Case tree. There, in its
broad, strong branches, soothed by a leaf lullaby,
they talked of all the wonderful things to come.

EPILOGUE

A small article appeared not long afterwards in
the *Greeley Times*.

Mystery in Greeley

Cecil Stromwold, owner of Cecil Stromwold's Stupendous
Circus, has disappeared, and circus employees suggest that
he has absconded with their paychecks. Greeley police, however, report that a large sum of money has been found in the
circus safe, along with two odd-looking unidentified nuts.

Earlier reports that Mr. Stromwold's clothes were discovered in the elephants' pen have been confirmed. "There is
no explaining why these clothes were left here," stated Chief
of Police Daryl Babcock.

The circus has been plagued by unfortunate mishaps. At
the same time as Mr. Stromwold's disappearance, an elephant stampede broke out in Mrs. Perry's field. It is believed
that it was caused by the untimely appearance of a mouse.
The Perry property has been badly torn up, but Mrs. Perry
says she will be planting corn there anyway.

The *Times* is happy to report that all of the circus animals have found loving homes.